MESSAGE
in the SNOW

Dawn Merriman

Dedication

This book is dedicated to my wonderful husband, Kevin and my children. Thank you for always supporting me. Also dedicated to all my fans. Your love of Gabby inspired me to write this book.

-Dawn Merriman

Chapter 1

GABBY

"Gabby, are you Daddy's girlfriend?" Olivia asks from the backseat of Lucas's car on our way home from Grandma Dot's Christmas Eve party.

The question unsettles me more than it should. After months, maybe even years, of dancing around our feelings, Lucas and I finally danced our way to each other. I've been labeled a lot of things in my life, freak, witch, even murderer and the devil. Girlfriend is a label I never expected to wear.

At only eight, labels make things easier for Olivia to understand. "I saw you two kissing. That means you're boyfriend and girlfriend, right?"

I can't fault the girl's logic. Lucas's hand on mine squeezes tighter. "Would you like it if Gabby was my girlfriend?" He asks his daughter.

My breath catches in my throat. It seems my whole world is riding on her answer. I'd rarely spent time with Lucas on his weekends with Olivia. Christmas Eve dinner at Grandma Dot's suddenly feels like some sort of relationship test. What if Olivia doesn't like me? Will that matter?

Olivia takes her time answering. I can see her face in the rear view mirror. Her eyes are squinting the same way Lucas's do when he's thinking hard. She feels me watching her, and meets my gaze in the reflection.

"I like you," she says through the mirror. "You make Daddy laugh. He needs to laugh more." The innocent remark sets my life back in balance.

"I like you, too," I say to her reflection. Olivia has already lost interest in the conversation and has gone back to the book

Grandma Dot gave her tonight.

I dare a glance at Lucas for his reaction. He's trying to keep himself from laughing, but loses the battle. A chuckle escapes his clenched lips.

"What's so funny?"

"You should have seen your face. Terrified of a little girl," he says so only I can hear.

"What if she didn't like me?"

"How could she not like you? You're wonderful." He lifts my hand and kisses the skin of my wrist exposed at the edge of my glove. "To answer her question, yes, you are my girlfriend. If that's okay with you."

I snuggle closer, mumbling. "Perfectly okay with me." The whole evening has been perfect. Grandma Dot finally got the Christmas Eve with her whole family that she has always wanted. My mom, finally released from prison, her innocence proven, was the best gift of all. Even my brother Dustin and his wife were pleasant.

"Did you see Alexis actually handed Walker to me and let me hold him?" I ask

Lucas. "Maybe she and I will become friends." I humph at the thought. "I mean it is Christmas. Miracles do happen."

Lucas kisses the top of my head. "You never know," he says vaguely. My brother Dustin is head detective of the River Bend, Indiana Police Department. He's not only Lucas's partner and best friend, but also sort of his boss. He's found it best not to get too involved with family squabbles. Alexis and I will just have to sort out our differences on our own terms, and leave the men out of it.

Fine with me. I prefer fighting my own battles the way I have my entire life.

The snow had been falling soft and pretty all evening, a lovely addition to the holiday. Now that it's fully dark, it starts blowing harsh against the windshield. The moon that had magically twinkled across the white fields before has been swallowed by clouds. In typical Indiana fashion, the weather is changing fast.

The shift in the atmosphere matches a shift in me. Suddenly jumpy and nervous, I push away from Lucas and sit up tall in my seat. I rub my gloved palms down my thighs, anxiety tingling in my legs.

Lucas switches on the wipers, and they squeak against the glass.

The sound brings back a memory of me tearing the wipers off of my Charger and throwing them across a wet parking lot. I shake my head to stop the memory and shove it back into the box where I keep all the terrors I've been through.

"What's wrong?" Lucas asks, his eye flitting quickly to Olivia in the back seat. "It's just snow."

"I'm not sure." I jam my palms against my thighs, to keep my hands from shaking. "I'm sensing something." I stare out the windows into the blowing snow. I scan the side of the road and the edges of fields and wooded areas lit by the car's headlights. I have no idea what I'm searching for. "Can you slow down?"

Used to my strange abilities, and trusting in my instincts, Lucas slows the car almost to a crawl.

"What are you looking for?" he asks.

"I don't know. I'm just, itchy, you know?"

He nods. He does know.

My left arm begins to tingle. On the inside of my left arm, a few inches below my elbow, I have a tattoo of a delicately drawn cross. Through the thickness of my winter coat, I rub my arm.

"What's going on?" Olivia asks.

"Be quiet for just a minute, Ollie-bug," Lucas says, his eyes locked on my hand rubbing my arm.

"Is Gabby having one of her psycho spells?" she asks.

"It's psychic, not psycho. And yes she is." Lucas tells her. "Please sit quietly."

"Mommy always calls it psycho," Olivia mutters.

Lucas watches me intently, his face a mix of cop curiosity and boyfriend concern.

The psycho comment has thrown my concentration off. I don't want to do this in front of Olivia. I don't want this tonight at all. It's Christmas Eve. Why can't I have a normal holiday, a normal life?

The jumpy, anxious feeling escalates. I want to fly out of the car, I want to hide from the message I know is coming. I want to run away from myself.

There's nowhere to run.

Lucas has stopped the car on the side of the road. Snow blasts past the beams of the headlights.

I stare at the blowing snow and breathe.

And listen for His instructions.

Turn around.

"We've already passed it. Turn the car around."

Lucas makes a quick three point turn and returns the way we came. The wipers work furiously at the blowing snow. A car passes us from the opposite direction driving slow in the snow. I search the side of the road, my anxiety creeping as our car creeps along the asphalt.

"Do you know what we are looking for?" Lucas whispers.

I shake my head, concentrating. "He just said turn around."

The tingle in my tattoo grows unbearable. "It really stings, we have to be close," I say desperately.

"There." Lucas points at the side of the road.

"I don't see anything." I press my nose to the cold glass of my window, wipe away the fog created by my breath.

"There's a gap in the snow. Looks like tire tracks."

Olivia leans forward, concerned by our tones. "Daddy, what's happening?"

"Just sit tight Ollie-bug. I need to go check on something." He's already undoing his seat belt, reaching into the glove compartment for his gun belt and tools.

"Police stuff?" Olivia whines, sitting back in her seat with a hard humph. "It's always police stuff."

"Just stay here and do not get out of this car." Lucas commands his daughter as he straps on his police gear. "Understand."

"Yes," Olivia says. "I know the drill."

I barely hear the last of her words, as I'm

already out of the car. The wind whips the hood of my coat and blows my dark curls into my face. I tuck my hair into the hood and pull the string tight, tying it into a bow under my chin. I pull the zipper as high as it will go. Protected as much as possible against the growing storm, I follow the tracks Lucas spotted.

This side of the road falls steeply away then flattens out. The land beyond is choked with brush and a few trees. Two tracks, barely visible in the blowing snow, slide down the bank and into the brush.

Lucas's flashlight bounces behind me, but I don't wait for him. My dress boots aren't made for hiking down a snowy bank. After about two steps, I slide on my rear to the bottom of the hill.

"You okay?" Lucas calls against the wind.

I jump up and follow the tracks into the brush, not hearing him. I can only hear the one word repeated by my tattoo.

Hurry.

Chapter 2

GABBY

The tracks clearly show a vehicle skidded down the bank, picked up speed and disappeared into the brush. Some of the brush is broken and scattered, but a lot of the branches closed back in behind the vehicle. I have to duck under and push against the branches to follow the tracks. One nasty vine of thorns catches on the hood of my coat and traps me.

"If you'd wait for me, I could help you," Lucas says, as he untangles the thorny vine.

"I can't wait. All I can hear is 'hurry'."

"Well, getting yourself hurt in the process won't help anyone. At least take my light."

"A light would help. Where's my phone?" I dig my phone out of my pocket and turn on the flashlight feature. I scan through the brush, following the tracks.

The beam glints off chrome a few yards away. "There's the car!" I run ahead, oblivious to the clinging vines and branches.

The car may have picked up speed from careening down the bank, but a tree caused a sudden stop. The front end on the driver's side is crumpled around the tree. The red metal of the hood looks like crinkled tissue paper wrapped around the dark brown tree trunk. Broken branches and chips of paint dot the snow like confetti.

I trudge through the snow as quickly as possible to the driver's window, hoping against hope we're not too late.

The window is broken, but still intact. The spider web pattern of shattered glass and the snow blocks my view of the driver. Lucas is talking on his radio and simultaneously, hollering at me over the wind.

"Gabby, be careful. Wait for me." I rub my glove against the window, trying to clear the snow and see through the broken pane. The inside of the car is dark. I hold up my phone light and peer into the car.

A man's head leans against the window, his temple flattened at the center of the cracked glass. Blood dribbles from his slack mouth and from his nostrils, bright red against the pale of his skin.

I fumble with the door handle, anxious to get to the man. The door is hopelessly stuck, a mess of wrinkled metal.

Lucas takes me by the shoulders and turns me away from the scene, expecting to comfort me. I don't need comfort. I need to act. My senses are zinging and the *hurry* is still screaming in my head. The driver is already beyond our help.

He's not why I was called here.

I push away from Lucas and slip and slide around the car. The back door on this side is hanging open, but a quick look inside shows there's no one in that seat. I reach the passenger door. Lucas is shining his light on the dead man on the other side of the car. A human shaped lump of shadow leans against the passenger window.

I cling to the door handle, the metal so cold it penetrates my thin gloves. I pull the handle, and the door creaks open.

A woman tumbles against me, barely conscious and held in the car by her seat belt. I hold her upright, her head drops onto my shoulder, her ice cold cheek brushes against mine.

"Run, kids," she mumbles into my ear.

"She's alive," I shout. "We're not too late."

The beam of Lucas's flashlight fills her face, searches her body. Thank God, all of her limbs seem to be intact or at least in place. While I hold her up, he leans into the car and unhooks her seat belt. Lucas pulls the woman from the bashed car and sets her on the snow. He kneels next to her, while I look on, unsure what to do to help. "The ambulance is already on its way," he tells her. "Just hang on."

The woman's eyes flutter open and lock on mine. "Save my kids."

The woman's eyes flutter again but remain closed, her face calm. "Stay with me, now." Lucas tells her.

I step away from the woman and the first aid Lucas is administering to her. The whole scene feels wrong. Car crashes happen every day, but something about this one is making my senses zing.

The open back door creaks as the wind blows against it.

"The back door's open," I shout to Lucas.

"Probably popped open on impact. Can you check on the man?"

"He's dead," I say flatly. I don't need to touch him, I can tell from here. "He died on impact."

I climb into the back seat. An empty baby car seat and booster seat fill most of the space. A few toys and other kid's things are on the floor. A small pink bear with unbelievably large eyes looks up at me. I pick up the bear, smoothing the hot pink fur with the tip of my black gloved finger. The bear's huge eyes seem to beg me for answers I don't have. I place it back on the floor, face down, so it will stop looking at me.

Squeezed next to the car seat, I open my

mind and listen.

Laughing, joking, holiday merriment. Five voices.

"Gabby," Lucas barks. "I could use some help, here."

"I'm working," I shout back, annoyed he broke my contact.

I take off my left glove and from the backseat, I touch the dead man's shoulder.

Headlights too close. What the--. The hill, the brush, the tree.

"They were run off the road on purpose," I tell Lucas. "Someone was following way too close and forced them off the road and down the bank."

"I don't even need to ask how you know that, do I?"

Far in the distance, carried by the wind, sirens sing. "The ambulance is coming." I begin to climb out of the back seat, still disturbed, still jumpy. Maybe it's the lingering, recent death of the man.

With my bare left hand, I touch the door handle on my way out.

Screaming, children screaming. Run kids. Don't take the road, they'll find you. Run, before they come back. Indecision. Mom's hurt, but she said go. Three different hands touch the handle on the way out into the winter storm. Small hands.

I slam back in the seat, shocked by the strength of the vision. I touch the car seats, touch the toys and kids items strewn about. Three children. An older boy, about Olivia's age, a girl about five and a boy not much older than Walker.

"Her children are out here!" I shout to Lucas. "They were in the car during the wreck. She told them to run."

Lucas scans the brushy area with his high powered flashlight for any sign of the kids. "Are you sure? I don't see any footprints or anything."

"The wind's been blowing like crazy. We were lucky to see the tire tracks, let alone tiny footprints in the snow."

"Why would she tell them to run?" He doesn't doubt what I saw, only doubts the woman's choices.

"She said run and hide before they come back. That's all I know."

I'm hopping around and anxious to begin searching. Lucas reads my mind. "Don't go running off into the dark by yourself. The ambulance is almost here. Dustin's on his way as well as some patrol officers. We can launch a search as soon as we get a party together."

I pull the collar of my coat tighter under my chin. "But it's freezing out here and any trace of the kids is blowing away in the wind as we speak."

I've already started into the brush, following my instincts but searching for footprints. "Gabby, please. I'm begging you to wait for backup."

I spin and face him. "Lucas, I love you dearly, but I have to do things the way I do them. The only backup I've ever had is God." I hold up my left, tattooed, arm. "Right now he's telling me to go."

A pained look distorts his face. I've crossed a line and I know it. "Do what you're gonna do. I can't stop you anyway." We stare at each other for a few tense moments. I know I've screwed up, but don't know how to fix it, not right now. I turn, thinking the conversation is over. "God may always have your back," Lucas calls after me, "But don't forget who's always been here right next to you."

Detective Lucas Hartley, that's who.

He's saved my life on more than one occasion. He's saved my heart.

I almost turn around and throw myself at his feet, beg for his forgiveness for my loose tongue.

The lights and sirens are closer now and a crush of people will soon swarm the scene.

I'll have to apologize later. Right now, I have three missing children to find.

I open my mind to the universe and listen. A nudge to the right here and a press to the left there, I follow the trail only I can feel. Now and again, I find a series of depressions in the snow that look like footprints only half filled in with blown snow. Tiny signs that I'm on the right path.

The chill of the icy blast blows up the back of my coat. I wrap my arms tighter across my waist to block the cold out. My fingers sting with cold, the thin gloves I always wear are no match for the frigid weather. I think of the children and how cold their tiny bodies must be.

Far behind me, the bright lights of the first responders glow against the low hanging clouds. Soon, a team will be sent to help me find the kids. I break branches on purpose, marking my trail to help them follow me.

That's if I'm even headed in the right direction. My senses aren't foolproof. Maybe I just want to believe I can find them, want to believe I can be a hero.

Maybe I'm fooling myself.

I duck under a stand of pine trees that offers some protection against the wind. Several footprints are easily seen here. The kids had taken shelter under these pines as well. I have no idea how long of a head start they have on me. How long their mom laid broken and bleeding before we found her. I shout for them, hoping they are close by.

The wind howls in response. Two sets of prints wander from under the pine tree. The older boy must be carrying the toddler.

It reminds me of the "Footprints in the Sand" plaque Grandma Dot has hanging in her bathroom. A poem about how God carries us when we need it most. I say a quick prayer that he's carrying the kids now and carrying me to them.

After breaking a large branch from the pine tree to direct the police search team, I follow in the direction of the kids.

My tattoo sizzles with pain so hot I cry out in pain.

Faster, run, hurry.

I push against the vines and branches, jog through the open areas. "I'm going as fast as I can," I yell into the wind. "I'm doing my best."

The light on my phone only illuminates so far, and the pale moonlight doesn't help much under the trees. I don't see any more footprints or other signs of the kids. Desperate now, I crash along, hoping my feet will find the right path.

The moonlight behind the trees grows brighter, where the wooded area gives way to an open field.

Almost there, run.

I shove my phone in my pocket and sprint as fast as I can for the edge of the woods. In the dim light, I don't see the wire fence line. The ancient fence has been smooshed to only a few feet tall, and is buried in years of leaves and fallen branches.

The top wire hits me just above my knees and I fall flat on my face in the snow. It takes me a moment to realize what happened. I lift my face from the snow and look across the open field.

Far across the field two shadows hurry. One small shape that must be the girl and an awkwardly shaped one that must be the older boy carrying the toddler.

Still lying in the snow, I scream for the kids, but they're too far away to hear me

With my eye locked on the shadows, I

scramble to get up. The barbed wire at the top of the fence has caught on my jeans. I shake my leg, kicking to get free. The rusty wire digs into my skin.

I look away from the kids and concentrate on releasing my leg from the barb. Finally free, I jump up and run through the snow.

We've travelled one country block and the next road north of the wreck site cuts through the fields near the kids. Headlights cut through the blowing snow on that road. The car is driving slowly, too slowly even considering the weather.

I sprint as fast as I can through the field, the snow and the corn stubble beneath catching on my dress boots.

"Wait," I yell into the wind.

The car stops near the kids.

I pound as fast as I can. I jog at the park regularly, so I'm in fairly good shape, but soon my lungs ache and my legs burn. I don't give in to my weakness. My tattoo urges me forward.

The driver gets out of the car and waves to

the kids.

Everything in me screams, "Don't do it!"

The driver looks up suddenly, as if they heard me, then focuses back on the kids.

The children hurry to the driver. The older boy hands the toddler to the driver, then helps his sister up the small bank of weeds at the edge of the field.

I continue to run, panicked, desperate to stop the kids from leaving. Gasping and struggling through the snow, I watch the kids climb into the car willingly.

Nothing seems dangerous. The kids don't seem scared.

The car pulls away, driving much faster than it was when it arrived.

The kids are gone.

They should be safe.

My entire body screams, "No!"

With no reason to keep running, I fall to my knees in the snow.

The tingling of my tattoo has stopped.

The hurry, faster, run, in my head has stopped.

The wind has even stopped.

I kneel alone in the center of the field. A heavy cloud covers the moon and the stars. It's so dark, I can barely see anything.

Tears of frustration and shame squeeze out of the corners of my eyes. I wipe angrily at them. Stickers and thorns and various pieces of the woods have snagged onto my thin cotton gloves, and scratch my face.

I deserve the pain, deserve the scratches.

It looks like the kids are now safe.

I know they're not. I was too late. I didn't save them.

Whoever ran their car off the road, killing that man and probably their mother has the kids.

She told them to run. She told me to save them.

The kids ran, but I didn't save them.

Chapter 3

LUCAS

I'm not surprised when Gabby runs off into the freezing woods alone. She's the most stubborn and impulsive woman I've ever known.

And dangerous. She's right, God does guide her, but I've had to help her out of serious scrapes on more than one occasion. If she'd just listen to me once in a while, or let me help her, it would be better for everyone.

But if she did that, she wouldn't be Gabby. I might as well try to stop the wind from blowing. I'd get the same result as trying to control Gabby.

The EMTs soon appear and take over caring for the injured woman. After her few muttered words, she has been quiet. Her pulse is steady and her breathing is steady. Her head is bleeding, but it looks like the air bag may have taken the worst of the impact.

With the EMTs in charge, I step away from the crushed car and survey the rest of the scene. Gabby said the car was run off the road on purpose. The tracks down the bank from the road do match that scenario.

The car seats and things in the back seat make it obvious that there had been kids in the car at some time. The woman did mention kids.

Who would run an entire family off the road on purpose on Christmas Eve?

I'm so focused on surveying the scene I don't notice Dustin until he's at my side.

"What've you got so far?" my best friend and partner asks.

I fill him in on the few details I have. Dustin's shoulders rise in tension as I explain how we came to find the wreck in the first place and how Gabby knows about the car being forced down the bank and into the trees.

"Leave it to my sister," he grumbles. He scans the scene. "Where is she, anyway?"

I hadn't told him that part yet, knowing he'd be angry. Angry at her for running off and angry at me for letting her go alone. I explain what happened and Gabby's theory about the missing children.

Dustin huffs in disapproval. He's tried hard the last month or so to be more understanding about his sister and how she operates. His brush with death put things in perspective, I guess.

Dustin starts barking orders. Technically, he's still on medical leave and not on duty, but that doesn't stop him from taking charge. As other officers join the scene, he puts together a search party.

"Gabby McAllister has gone off this way," Dustin motions with his arm that's still in a sling from being shot a few weeks ago, "Supposedly to find three children that ran away from the scene."

A few grumbles filter through the group at the mention of Gabby. Dustin's tone and 'supposedly' doesn't help matters any.

I step up and take over. "Just before the

woman victim lost consciousness, she asked Gabby to find her children." The group quiets and takes the situation more seriously. "She started off in that direction. Judging by the items in the car, we are looking for a baby, a preschooler and an older child."

The team starts off into the trees and brush. I'm anxious to go with them, but Olivia is still alone in my car up on the road. "Is Alexis and Walker with you?" I ask Dustin.

"She dropped me off and headed home." Dustin looks towards the road. "You still have Olivia up there, don't you?" He pulls his phone out of his pocket.

"Would she mind?"

"Not at all. She gets it."

After a short conversation with Alexis, he hangs up. "She'll be here in a few minutes."

I hate to put off searching for Gabby, but I have to put my daughter first right now. I push through the brush and up the bank to my car.

Olivia is sitting in the back seat, her head leaning against the window. Amidst all the lights and activity, she's fallen asleep. My heart hurts looking at her. I'm surprised as I always am at the massive rush of love that courses through me. She is the most precious thing.

And I've left her on the side of the road at a crime scene on Christmas Eve.

She deserves better.

I open the back door and slide in next to her. The running car is overly warm after kicking around in the blowing snow in my dress coat and slacks. The sudden gust of cold and my presence wakes her.

She opens her eyes and leans sleepily against my shoulder. "Can we go home now?" she asks. "Santa's coming."

"We can't go home yet, Ollie-bug. But how about you go with Aunt Alexis and Walker and wait for Santa there?"

She pushes away from my shoulder. The tiny space of air between us stings.

"You're not coming with me? But it's Christmas." She fights to keep the whine out of her voice.

"I know, baby. I'm really sorry. But

someone got hurt down there. And some little kids got lost in the snow storm. I have to stay and help find them."

"Can Gabby take me home? We can wait for you at your house."

I think about my answer for a moment. "Well, see, Gabby went out looking for the missing kids already. We're kind of looking for her, too."

Olivia sits fully upright. The tilt of her chin reminds me of her mom, Amber. The space of air between us grows. "Did she have another one of her psycho things?" Her sweet voice has a hard edge to it now.

"It's psychic, and yes, something like that." How do I explain Gabby to an eight year old? "Gabby sensed the kids were in trouble, so she went to help. That's what Gabby does. She helps people."

"Then she should be a cop like you," Olivia says sensibly.

"We all help people in our own way." Alexis's minivan pulls close to my car, saving me from a deeper discussion. "Look, Olivia,

I'm really sorry. I truly am. But think of the little kids out there in the cold. It's Christmas for them, too. At least you'll be safe and warm with Alexis and Walker."

Olivia opens her door. I think for a minute she's going to climb out of the car without another word. She stops, though, thinking. She suddenly throws her arms around my neck.

"Go save those kids, Daddy. And find Gabby. I hope they're all okay." She snuggles her face into my neck and my heart melts.

"Merry Christmas," I whisper into her ear.

Alexis appears and helps Olivia out of the car. Dustin's wife's eyes meet mine. A mixture of sorrow and annoyance with a heavy dose of resigned acceptance fills her expression.

"Thanks for coming back to get her," I say lamely.

Alexis shrugs. As a cop's wife, she's used to the sacrifices. "We all have to help each other," she says the words, but there's little conviction behind them. She looks at Olivia, "Uncle Dustin called Santa and told him you would be staying at our house tonight, so don't you worry."

Olivia beams at me. "Did you hear that?"

"I did. Now you better get there and go to bed so he can come." To Alexis, I mouth, "Thank you."

She gives me a small smile, and shuts the car door.

I take a short moment alone in the overly heated car to switch mental gears. I reach over the back seat and turn off my car. As I reach, I step on something hard on the back floor board. It's the book Grandma Dot gave Olivia tonight. I pick up the book and wipe the dirty snow off on my pants. The cover comes clean, but I've bent it so badly, a crease cuts through the face of the puppy on the front.

I stare at the ruined book, a physical symbol of Olivia's ruined Christmas. "Don't screw this up this year," Amber had said to me when I picked Olivia up yesterday. "She's old enough to remember things like a ruined holiday now."

I'd glared in frustration at my ex-wife then, sure she was exaggerating. "I think I can handle a Christmas," I'd said as evenly as my damaged pride would allow.

"Let's hope so." Resentment seethed behind her words, but she quickly changed to all smiles as Olivia joined us on the front porch.

I rub at the broken book as if my touch could return it to the perfect condition it was in only hours ago when Olivia unwrapped it. I'll have to ask Grandma Dot where she got it and replace it before Olivia sees the damage.

"You have bigger things to worry about than a puppy book right now," I say out loud, giving myself a mental shake. I shove the book far under the car seat for now.

I've done the best I can for Olivia right now.

One girl I love is safe and warm.

Now I need to find the other one.

With all the fresh footprints from the search team, it's tricky to know which way to go through the woods. I start in the direction I'm pretty sure Gabby went in. Several yards in, I find a what looks like a recently broken branch.

"That's my smart girl," I mutter. "Mark the trail."

The wind had been quiet for the few minutes I was in the car, but it has picked back up and blasts even harder now. The snow has changed from flakes to tiny chips of stinging ice. They blow sideways, stinging my bare cheeks. My ears strain to hear the shouts or whistles or some signal the children have been found. I only hear the wind and the ice hitting the ground.

I try calling Gabby on her cell, but she doesn't answer. Until now, I've kept my concern on the kids, trusting Gabby to keep herself safe. When she doesn't answer her phone, I increase my pace.

Can't hear the phone in this wind, that's all.

The search party has spread out through the brush and trees, obviously missing the broken branches I've been following. The team had taken off in pairs, I find myself alone with my growing fear. Are these broken branches even from her? Maybe an animal broke them, or the weight of the snow. I wish I had a tattoo to guide me the way Gabby does.

I only have my instincts. I trudge on, following the path I'm fairly certain she took.

The light grows beyond the edge of the trees, indicating a field. With my powerful flashlight, I follow what looks like Gabby's foot prints until I reach a half-downed wire field fence.

A patch of snow on the other side of the fence is flattened. It looks like someone tripped over the fence and fell into the snow.

The tiniest of smiles crosses my lips. Gabby has a way of acting without thinking, tripping and falling in her enthusiasm. The marks in the snow are definitely hers.

A tiny piece of denim fabric clings to one of the sharp points on the barbed wire. I pluck the fabric and tuck it into my pocket.

After carefully climbing over the fence, I scan the field with my light. The beam only reaches so far into the snow covered corn stubble, but I can see a line of footprints in the snow. Flashlights are helpful in the dark, but they also make it harder to see beyond the beam.

I switch off the light and wait until my eyes adjust to the dark. Off to my left I see two officers searching the ground. Far across the field, on the next country road, I see a bump that looks out of place.

The bump moves.

My heart sinks as I recognize the shape of the bump even in the dark. Gabby is on the road.

Following her prints in the snow, I sprint across the field as fast as I can. I radio that I've found Gabby, but direct the search party to keep looking for the kids.

The blood pounds in my ears as I run and my dress shoes slide through the snow. The bump on the road continues to move. That's a good thing. If she's been hit by a car or something, at least she's still alive.

As I grow closer, I realize that the shape is Gabby on her hands and knees.

"Gabby," I shout once I'm close enough for her to hear over the blasting wind.

She looks up guiltily, but doesn't stand.

I climb through the weeds at the edge of the field. "What are you doing in the road? Are you hurt?"

Her face is full of misery, but not physical pain.

"I lost them," she says wildly. "They were right here and someone took them."

I crouch next to her, turn my light back on and scan the road. "What are you looking for?" I ask gently.

"I'm not looking. I'm trying to sense where they went or who took them."

Gabby only senses things with her left hand, but she has both of her gloves off. She's frantically pressing her palms into the icy asphalt. By her desperate state, I don't have to ask if she's getting anything.

"They're gone. Someone pulled over and they got into the car. I ran as fast as I could to save them, but I was too late."

"If someone picked them up, then they're

safe." I touch her shoulder, trying to soothe her.

"But they're not. Whoever their mom told them to run from is the same person who picked them up."

She's still on her hands and knees in the road. Luckily at this time of night on a holiday, there's no traffic.

"You don't know that for sure," I say. Her head snaps up with anger. I regret the words instantly. "I mean, you never know, maybe the mom was wrong and the kids are perfectly fine," I back-pedal.

"I know they're not fine." She shoves her bare hands onto the snowy road again. "If I could just get something, who the person was, what they wanted with the kids. Anything."

I pull her hands off the ground and rub them between my heavy gloves. "You're freezing." I blow warm air on her hands. A tip of her finger touches my lips. It's ice cold. "You've done all you can. Thanks to you, we know the kids aren't out here lost in the snow somewhere."

The tension in her shoulders slips a little. I push my advantage and help her to her feet and into the weeds. There might not be much traffic, but I need her out of the road. "We can call off the search and all these officers can get out of this storm." I continue talking and leading her further into the field.

I pull off my gloves and slip them onto her red fingers. Then I pull her tight against my chest. Wearing my dress coat, I'm not exactly prepared for a winter storm either, but my recent sprint across the field has warmed me up. I unzip my coat and slide her arms around my waist, all the while talking softly and slowly.

Her arms are like ice tentacles wrapped around my middle. She pushes her face against my chest and I can feel the cold of her cheek through my shirt. "We'll find the kids," I tell her. "I promise."

The tension in her body releases a little more and she leans against me. "I tried so hard," she whispers.

"I know you did." I kiss the top of her

hooded head. "This storm's really kicking up. We have to get out of this weather."

Gabby suddenly springs upright and searches my face. "Where's Olivia?" she asks in a panic. I'm touched by her concern for my daughter, but not surprised.

"Alexis took her home with her."

Gabby sags against me. "Crap on a cracker. That means Dustin's here."

I nod, biting back a smile.

She unwinds her arms from inside my coat and starts retracing her steps through the field.

"I can call a car to come pick us up, you know?" I say following her.

"Dustin's going to throw a fit at me. Walking will take longer and postpone the lecture." Her shoulders are thrown back and her chin is up. She looks nothing like the desperate broken woman that was pawing at the road a few minutes ago.

I match my stride to hers. "You know he only acts like that because he worries about you."

"So I've been told. Doesn't change the fact

that he can be a real pain. I may be his younger sister, but I'm not a child."

We walk a few paces in silence.

"Don't you dare say that out loud," she says suddenly.

My cheeks burn against the cold air. "Say what?"

"That I may not be a child but I act like one sometimes."

I stop in my tracks. That's exactly what I was thinking.

Gabby breaks into a loud laugh. "I was just guessing, I didn't read your mind or anything."

I look at her, unsure.

"I was thinking that sometimes, maybe, I do act like a child." She flashes a glance in my direction. "Only makes sense you would have been thinking it, too."

"Aren't we all just kids on the inside? Scared kids trying to play grown up?"

Gabby stops suddenly and looks me straight in the face. "That is the smartest thing anyone has ever said," she whispers. She then leans in slowly, and touches her lips to mine.

Alone in the snowy field on Christmas Eve, the scene is almost romantic and I can forget the reason we're out here. We take advantage of the moment.

All the worry and frustration of the last hour pours out of me in that kiss. Gabby matches my intensity. When we finally pull apart, she tips her forehead to my chest.

"I can hear your heart beating," she says. "It's going pretty fast."

"Well, I have been traipsing all over the wilderness tonight," I tease.

She tips her head back and gives me a special look, "Is that all?"

I drop my head to kiss her again. Dustin's voice rattles out of my radio. "Hartley, are you and Gabby almost back? We have an ID on the victims."

I grab my radio and answer. "We're headed that way." I pull away from Gabby, giving her a *hopefully later* look. We start walking across the field again. "Wait, did you say victims, plural?"

Dustin's voice is somber as he says, "The

woman died en route. If what you say about them being forced off the road is true, we have a double homicide."

"And a kidnapping," Gabby adds.

The snowy field is no longer romantic. A different kind of passion burns in me as we retrace our steps through the woods.

Chapter 4

GABBY

Maybe he's too busy dealing with the case or maybe it's a Christmas miracle, but Dustin doesn't chew me out when Lucas and I get back to the wrecked car. His sharp blue eyes take in every detail from my tightly tied hood, to the tear in my jeans from the barbed wire fence. Satisfied that I'm okay or at least not going to cause him any immediate trouble, he shifts back into cop mode.

"The driver was Eric Landry," Dustin says, checking his notes. "Dead on the scene."

As if we didn't know that part already. I'm more surprised at the woman's passing. Lucas shares my concerns.

"The woman was stable when I was with her," Lucas says. "Well, maybe not stable, but her breathing was regular, her heartbeat was steady. What happened?" The pain and disappointment seeps past his attempt at official detachment. "She wasn't even bleeding. The air bag took most of the impact."

Dustin doesn't have an answer. "They just said she died on the way to the hospital. I guess we'll know more later."

Lucas looks at me for any insights. "Did you pick anything up from her? It doesn't make sense that she died."

I can only shrug helplessly. "I didn't really touch her or anything. I was more focused on her kids."

"What was her name?" Lucas asks. "Who was she?"

"Lauren Whitlow. We ID'd both victims by their driver's licenses. That's all we have at the moment."

"Different last names," I point out. "Boyfriend?"

"Likely," Dustin says. "We're still working on names and ages for the kids, but we'll have that info soon. Any other info on the car that picked them up?"

I look with shame at the heavy gloves covering my hands. "I didn't get anything new. Just a light colored four door sedan."

Lucas blows air hard in exasperation. A shiver shakes his shoulders.

"Why don't we get out of this storm for now," I offer. "Then figure out our next move."

Dustin looks at me sharply, "We?"

"Yes, *we.* I'm part of this. If it wasn't for me, you wouldn't even have found this car or known about the missing kids."

"I'm so sick of the 'if it wasn't for me' line," he grumbles. He says it under his breath, but I hear it anyway.

"Sorry to be such a help," I snide back.

"Just knock it off," Lucas snaps as if he's correcting fighting children.

Dustin and I are both knocked speechless from his harsh tone.

"Two people have died and three children are missing." Lucas's chest heaves with frustration. "And you two are squabbling like children."

Dustin and I both raise our chins in identical expressions. "Sorry," I grumble. "You're right."

Lucas takes charge of the situation. "Gabby, you take my car and go home. Dustin and I will ride back with the other officers and pick up our cruiser."

I want to argue, to bristle at being told to go home, but Lucas holds up his hand before I can form the words.

"We have to go inform some family members that their loved ones were killed on Christmas Eve," he says, his voice breaking. "Whatever you're about to say isn't important compared to that."

Lucas turns suddenly and stalks through the brush, following the tire tracks back to the road.

"He's pretty upset," I say to my brother. "I've never seen him like that."

Dustin kicks his dress shoes at the snow and rubs his slinged arm. "I have," he says softly. "You wouldn't understand." He follows Lucas up the tracks.

I don't take offense at the words and match pace with him. "Yes, I guess I can't understand." I can't imagine what they go through on a daily basis. I can only be thankful for them. "He's right about the woman. Lauren Whitlow? There's something fishy about that. She was banged up, but she didn't seem that bad. Will there be an autopsy or anything?"

"Normally, not, but I can order one."

I nod, thinking about Lauren Whitlow and what she was so afraid of. I finally give words to my fears, "Do you think the kids are okay?" I ask my brother. "They went willingly into the car that found them. But why was someone looking for them? Who would even know they were out here to be found. It had to be the same person who forced them off the road."

Dustin takes pity on me. "Whoever has them probably won't hurt them. Most likely their father took them. Family abductions rise sharply at the holidays."

The thought gives me a little hope. "He wouldn't hurt his own kids, then, right?"

"Let's hope not." He raises his damaged

arm, reminding me how he got the gunshot that put him in the sling. Some fathers are capable of anything. Despite our differences, Dustin and I share that fact.

We've almost reached the road, a few more steps through the brush and we'll be visible. Lucas impatiently waits for us, talking to another officer, making plans. I touch Dustin's sleeve, stopping him. "He's pretty upset," I say, nodding to Lucas. "Keep an eye on him."

Dustin surprises me by wrapping his good arm around my shoulders. "I always do." The tender moment is fleeting, but infinitely warm.

He drops his arm and hurries up the bank, leaving me wondering if I'd imagined the half-hug.

When I reach Lucas, he has deep lines on his face and his lips are tight. "Can you take my car?" he asks. "And can you do me a massive favor?"

"Anything for you." I add a wide smile, hoping to take the edge off the last several minutes. He doesn't return the smile.

"Olivia went home with Alexis, but all her

presents are still at my house," he starts.

"Say no more," I interrupt him. "I'll take them to Dustin's for you. Can't have her thinking Santa forgot about her." I plaster on another smile. Lucas doesn't take the bait. His mind is on the awful news he has to deliver tonight.

"Keys are in the car," he says with barely a glance at me. I've been dismissed. He turns away, and takes a step towards the cruiser waiting for him. A guilty rush of jealousy flows into my blood. I have no idea what I feel jealous of. I don't envy what he has to do the rest of the night. I don't really want to be there when they deliver the death notices. The ugly jealousy remains.

I watch him climb into the back seat of the cruiser, the whole time expecting him to say something else to me, make some remark to let me know we're okay. He's in full cop mode, his mind on a million other things.

The cruiser door shuts and my boyfriend and my brother pull away. A few cars are still on scene and a few officers are still working on their various jobs, but I feel alone. I recognize the jealousy for what it really is.

The familiar ache of emptiness.

The icy snow blasts my face and a chill climbs into my chest.

"Merry Christmas," I whisper to the fading tail lights of the cruiser. This evening started off with so much promise. The lovely party at Grandma Dot's, my mom finally out of prison and with the family, and Lucas by my side. It had been the best Christmas I ever remembered.

I shiver against the blowing wind. My best jeans are soaked from climbing through the snow and torn from my battle with the barbed wire. The skin underneath stings where the wire cut me. My toes are frozen and wet inside my dress boots. I still wear Lucas's oversized gloves, but my fingertips burn with cold.

At least on Christmas' past, I wasn't standing alone freezing and wet on the side of the road.

I push the selfish thought away. Lauren Whitlow and Eric Landry will never have another Christmas. Those three kids probably won't have gifts waiting under any tree in the morning. If they even see the morning.

The morbid thought gets my feet moving. Lucas and Dustin work in their way, I work in mine. I may have been dismissed in an official capacity, but that hasn't ever stopped me before.

But first, I need to play Santa.

That thought makes my stomach sink. It means I'll have to see Alexis.

"Crap on a cracker," I mutter as I climb into Lucas's car. "You just ran off into the woods during a snowstorm without flinching. Seeing your sister-in-law alone should be a piece of cake."

I'd rather just eat the cake.

Chapter 5

GABBY

Driving Lucas's car feels oddly like a violation of his personal space. Maybe it's because I rarely let anyone drive my old Charger. I'm pretty sure Lucas doesn't have that kind of unhealthy attachment to his car. Thinking of my Dodge Charger, I decide to make a quick stop at my house first. In these dress clothes and Lucas's car, I don't feel like myself.

Chester, my gray and white cat, is pleased to see me, as always. Earlier, before Lucas picked me up for Grandma Dot's, I'd had a private celebration with Chester. I'd given him an entire can of tuna, served on the fanciest plate I owned. I'd seen something similar on those cat food commercials where the fancy cat gets fed on fine china, complete with a sprig of green garnish. My clear glass plate was far from fine china, but Chester didn't seem to mind. He rubs himself extra excitedly against my legs now, no doubt hoping for more tuna.

"You've already had your holiday treat," I tell him. He puts his front paw ups on my leg and looks up at me with the largest, begging eyes. "You're hopeless," I say and rub him between the ears. "Tell you what, I'll let you lick the can."

If I'd had another can of tuna, I'd gladly given it to him, but I'd only had the one. After digging the can out of the trash, I put a little bit of water in it and swish it around to catch the stray pieces of fish for him. No fancy plate for him this time, I simply set the can on the kitchen floor. Chester makes small noises of contentment as he laps at the fishy water.

"You're so easy to please," I tell him. "Too bad everyone isn't like you."

I leave Chester to his late night snack and go to my room to strip off my soaked boots and ruined jeans. It's late, almost officially

Christmas. The thought makes me sad. I want to climb into my bed with Chester and pretend it's just a night like any other, not the greatest night of the year.

"No rest for the weary," I tell Chester who has followed me into my room, licking his lips. "Or is it no rest for the worried? No rest for the weirdo? That sounds more like it."

I find some mostly clean jeans, dry hiking boots and a t-shirt. On a sudden inspiration, I remember a red hoodie Grandma Dot gave me years ago. I dig to the back of my closet and find it on a wire hanger. It's been hanging there so long, one shoulder is misshapen.

I pull the hoodie on and look in my dresser mirror. "What do you think?" I ask Chester.

The bright red hoodie has a hideous picture of Santa with a glittering beard checking his list. The shirt says, "I don't care what Santa thinks, I'd rather be naughty than nice." When Grandma Dot gave it to me three Christmas's ago, she'd laughed like it was some inside joke between us. I'd smiled politely, but didn't get it. Looking at it now, I still don't get it. I mean,

I *get it,* but I don't understand why Grandma thought it was a good gift for me.

"Does she think I'm naughty?" I ask my reflection. I guess looking back over the last year, maybe she's right. Either way, the huge red hoodie is the only holiday wear I have. It's thick and warm and bright and has lots of glitter and bling. After three years exiled to the far reaches of my closet, the glitter writing has started to come loose. A small shower of it drops to the carpet.

I'm too tired to care about the glitter. With a last pat for Chester, I zip my coat tight over the sweater, pull on a fresh pair of gloves and head back out into the cold. The blasting snow has stopped, but the cold bites at my nose and makes the hairs inside sting. I rub at my face, hating that particular sensation.

"Someday, I'm going to move where it's warm all the time," I grumble as I slide into my cold Charger. The freezing leather seats seep through my jeans and chill my rear. "I'm going to drive south and not stop," I continue as the heater battles with the chill. "Or maybe go out west. Anywhere there isn't snow."

I wipe at my tingling nose again, knowing full well I'll never leave River Bend. Everyone I love is here. That's how they get you, how they trap you. Why else would anyone want to live somewhere that's so cold?

I put the Charger in reverse, and continue grumbling. "That must be why the Canadians are all so nice to each other. Otherwise everyone would flee the weather."

I'm so tired, I chuckle at the lame joke. Driving through the deserted streets to Lucas's house, my eyes search for the car I saw pick up those kids. A light colored four door sedan is barely even a description. There has to be hundreds of them even in a town as small as River Bend.

I think hard about the car, try to remember any distinguishing features. Was there some sort of sticker on the back passenger window, or was that a smudge of snow? I focus hard on the memory. There had been a shape, but I can't be sure what I saw. I'd been so focused on the kids, I hadn't paid the car much attention. I can't even be sure if the person who took them was a man or woman.

"Not your best work tonight," I chastise myself as I pull into Lucas's driveway. In the front yard, a lighted blow up decoration of two penguins having a snowball fight has fallen victim to the storm. It's blown from the yard into the bushes by the front door. The light and fan are still running, but the penguins look like they belong in a Salvador Dali painting, melted and misshapen.

I pull the decoration out of the bushes and set it back up in the yard. The ground is too hard to drive the stakes back in, but one of them is still in the ground from before. I secure the penguins as best I can to the remaining stake.

I've never put Christmas lights or decorations up at my house. Vandals would have just torn them down, or worse. They don't hesitate to paint nasty words on my garage door or to toilet paper my trees, I can't imagine what they'd do to decorations I actually cared about.

I pat the smiling face of one of the penguins and imagine what it must be like to live a life like this. Where I could have something nice in my yard and not worry that some superstitious, hate-filled person would come wreck it. That dream is about as likely to come true as my dream of moving to where it's warm all the time.

Lucas had given me a key to his house a few weeks ago, a treasured piece of metal. I've never actually used it, have only been here with him.

I slide the cold key into the lock and turn, half expecting it to not work. The lock unlocks easily and the door swings open. The rush of warm air and the faint smell of his cologne invites me in. I don't need to turn on any lights, the Christmas tree lights fill the front room with a happy glow. It's so tall, it almost touches the ceiling. The tree at my house fits on my kitchen counter.

Being alone in Lucas's house feels even more like a violation against him than driving his car did. I'm not used to being part of a couple. I've known Lucas most of my life, and on some level have always cared for him, but this new "couple" dynamic is taking some getting used to.

I'm enjoying the getting used to it part, though.

Now that I'm at the house, I suddenly realize, I have no idea where Lucas hid Olivia's presents. She's too old to use the obvious places like his closet or under the bed. She's at that age where she's not quite sure Santa's still real, and might go snooping to prove her suspicions right. Knowing Lucas, he'd do everything he can to keep the fantasy alive as long as possible.

I don't want to go snooping myself either. Using my key to get in is one thing, but digging through his things without him here is another. I could text him and ask, but he's busy with actual hard work. I should be able to handle this small task without his help. I walk slowly around the dim house, wondering where he'd hide them. I try to think like him, like a parent. That's a jump of imagination I can't make.

The house isn't that big, there can't be too many places to look. I check the coat closet, the top shelf of the linen closet, even get desperate and look under his bed.

No presents.

I think back to when Dustin and I were kids and we did the inevitable snooping. Where had we looked? As I recall, Dustin always did the snooping, not me. I liked to be surprised by my gifts. He liked to know what was coming. Usually he'd find them without me, then tease me about knowing what I was getting and hold that knowledge over my head for days. One year, I'd desperately wanted one of those toy dogs that you could make bark and wag its tail. Dustin told me he'd found the stash and I wasn't getting one. I'd sulked for days and even secretly hoped Santa actually was real and would bring me one.

On Christmas morning, Dustin had been especially excited. He even grabbed the first gift and handed it to me. Confused, I'd taken the package wondering why he wore such a happy, expectant look.

As soon as I saw the fur in the package, I realized Dustin had lied about the dog toy.

"Surprised?" he asked with glee. "You said you wanted to be surprised. For once I didn't ruin it."

Mom seemed concerned, "Do you like it, Gabby? You've been begging for one for weeks."

I wasn't sure how to react. It was obvious Dustin meant well, hadn't wanted to ruin my surprise the way he had in years past. He'd been trying to be a good brother.

The surprise came at the expense of days of sulking, thinking my parents had ignored the one thing I truly wanted that year.

To cover my mixed reactions, I forced a wide smile to my face and squealed with pretend glee. "You really got me," I told Dustin as I tore at the paper. "My very own puppy," I said to my parents. "Thank you!"

Mom, Dad and Dustin all smiled real smiles. It should have been a perfect Christmas morning, a warm family memory.

I remember feeling duped. Dustin really was trying to be nice, but I felt like the butt of a bad prank. I played with the dog that day, because everyone expected me to. The next day, it 'accidentally' got shoved under my bed and I never touched it again. It had become a physical representation of Dustin's and my relationship. Even when he meant well, he hurt me. Even when he did something nice for me, I took it the wrong way. We were little kids then, but still the same now.

I pull my mind back from the memory. A few years later, our family had been torn to shreds by something much more important than me and my over-sensitive feelings about a gift. We survived that, so Dustin and I must be making progress somehow.

As soon as I find Olivia's gifts, I'm taking them to my brother's house. We may not be the best brother and sister, but at least we still have each other.

If I can find the stupid gifts.

Discouraged, I sit on Lucas's couch and look at the brightly lit tree. "Where did he hide them?" I ask the tree.

With my heavy hoodie and my coat on, I grow hot. I pull off my coat, and a trickle of glitter lands on my lap. "Crap on a cracker," I grumble brushing the glitter onto the carpet. "Wait, not on the carpet either." I can't stop the flutter of glitter onto Lucas's freshly vacuumed carpet. The only thing I can do is put my coat back on and zip it tight. I'll just have to be hot. I pull off a glove and start fanning my flushed face. The sight of my bare hand gives me an idea.

I've never used my gift for something like this. Rarely use it at all if I can avoid it.

Hoping God will forgive me, I hold up my bare left hand and think about the presents.

Nothing happens. Finding murder victims or saving people is one thing, but this?

"I'll be saving Olivia's Christmas," I rationalize. I stand up, hold my left hand high and open my mind to the universe. I don't question, I just follow the slight urges. I slowly make my way through the kitchen, shuffling my feet, my eyes squinted nearly closed. A solid metal door leads from the kitchen to the garage and my hand draws me to it.

With my left hand held in the air, I turn the knob with my right. The metal of the knob is cold, but the handle turns. The plastic, weather seal sticks and I have to shove my shoulder against the door to get it to open. Once it does, I shuffle into the dark garage. I find the light switch and the overhead flourescent bulbs hum to life.

I don't see any tell-tale bags or hidden piles that might be presents. A battered fridge hums to life and I jump slightly. Lucas keeps sodas and a few beers in this fridge. My mouth suddenly feels dry, thinking of the stash of Dr. Pepper or Cherry Pepsi he probably has in there for me. I take a break from looking for the gifts. He has both.

"Bless you," I say and take one of each. I stash a Dr. Pepper in the pocket of my coat and crack the top of the Cherry Pepsi. The hiss and the miniscule bubbles that escape fill me with more satisfaction than they should. The first drink from a fresh can is the best. The bubbles sting my nose and the sugar coats my tongue. I drink greedily, sighing afterward like they do in the commercials.

"You have a problem, you know," I say to myself, then take another deep drink. "Girl's gotta have a vice," I rationalize and down the rest of the soda.

I sneak another out of the fridge and put it in my other coat pocket. It might be a late night, and I might need the caffeine.

There's nothing else but a few shelves, some shovels and a lawn mower in the garage. Nothing that looks like gifts. I try anyway and lift my hand again and focus.

Feeling like the freak I'm often accused of being, I continue to scan my hand around the room, desperate for a clue.

The cable that hangs from the pull down steps to the attic bumps against my bare knuckles.

"Aha."

I wrap my hand around the cable and pull the steps down. They unfold into a rickety ladder leading to the black hole of the attic.

I'm not super fond of rickety steps, but the gifts have to be here, I've searched everywhere else. Halfway up the unstable ladder, I see two black plastic bags near the opening to the attic.

"Found you," I exclaim. Slightly ashamed, but also triumphant, I slide my gloves back on. Vowing to never tell anyone what I just did, I pull the bags of presents out of the attic and hastily fold the attic steps back up into the ceiling. They close with a bang.

"Good hiding spot, babe. Olivia can't even reach the cable to open the steps."

Proud of Lucas's hiding abilities and proud of my finding abilities, I drag the bags of gifts outside. I carefully lock up behind me. The blow-up penguins watch me load the heavy bags into the backseat of the Charger.

Judging by the amount of gifts in the two bags, Olivia must have chosen nice over naughty this year.

Chapter 6

GABBY

I had been impressed with Lucas's blow-up penguin decoration. Dustin's neighborhood puts that display to shame. Lucas and I both live in small houses in the older part of town. Dustin lives in one of the newer neighborhoods with curving streets with odd names like Cider Mill Run and Rainwater Cove. Each house struggles to be different, to stand out, but the houses end up all looking the same.

Christmas time is when the owners can really shine. The displays of lights here are spectacular, with each neighbor trying to outdo the next. Flashing and dancing stringers, automated figures that move, lightshows played out on rooftops and garage doors. Some even have music that the lights dance to. For most of December, people come from miles around and crawl through the streets, ogling at the light displays.

I can't imagine having the passion or energy to put up such displays. The electric bills alone must be higher than my mortgage.

This late at night, the lights are all on, dancing and flashing for all they're worth, but the streets are empty of cars. The brightest houses remind me of showgirls past their prime. Older women decked out in finery, dancing their hearts out to an empty room. I focus my eyes on the asphalt and not the blinking lights.

Most of these houses have young families in them. Lucky children are asleep in their rooms, sure of fabulous treats waiting for them in the morning.

I can only hope and pray the three missing children are safe somewhere, too.

One little girl in this neighborhood isn't in her own bed, not even her own house. I can't help the missing children right now, but I can help Olivia.

Dustin's house is at the far back of the neighborhood, his backyard borders a strip of undeveloped land. Beyond that is the sight of a new housing development that's being built, despite a major setback earlier in the fall. His street ends in a cul-de-sac, and the caravan of spectator cars rarely comes this far, so the displays are not as elaborate as the ones closer to the entrance.

Even so, it's obvious Dustin's is one of the few houses that have chosen not to compete in the unofficial lighting contest. His subdued strings tossed on the front bushes and candles in the front windows makes his house seem like the quiet girl in the corner compared to flashier dancing girl houses. It also has a homey, lived in, loved in feel. Something the large displays lack.

The wreath on his front door brings forth a wave of nostalgia. I haven't seen the circle of plastic greenery and fake pine cones since we were kids. Mom hung that same wreath on our door every year. The oversized red bow is a bit tattered now, the streaming ends blowing in the wind. I'd assumed the wreath had been thrown away at some point, hadn't really given it a thought since the night our lives shattered.

Dustin couldn't bring himself to visit our mother in prison, but he hung her wreath on his door. Does he hang it every year or did he dig it out of storage somewhere now that Mom is home? The fact that he hung onto the cheap display at all surprises me. Dustin's been doing a lot of things that surprise me lately.

Parked in his driveway with my headlights off, I realize I have a bigger dilemma than wondering about Dustin's wreath. I'd overlooked a small detail of this playing Santa gig I agreed to. I don't have a key to his house or Alexis' phone number. I could call Dustin to call Alexis, but it seems a tiny problem that I should be able to handle without interfering in their police work.

I could knock on the door, but that might wake the kids.

I could leave the bags of toys on the front step, but who knows when Dustin will be able to come home. If Olivia sees the bags on the step, any lingering childhood fantasy will be ruined for her.

"Crap on a cracker," I mutter. I open one of the sodas in my coat pockets and sip while I think. I try to think of a plan, not of how sad it is that I don't have my own sister-in-law's phone number. We've just started taking baby steps towards being friendly. We're a long way from the exchange-numbers-and-text-each-other-once-in-a-while stage.

I've only been inside Dustin's house one time, and that was a few years ago, but if my memory is correct, the window on the right goes to the master bedroom. I could knock on the window and wake Alexis.

That idea makes me think of scenes from romantic comedies where the lovesick male tosses rocks at his girlfriend's window. I can't picture myself in a romantic comedy, my life is more of a dark humor movie.

Deciding my best bet is to at least check if the doors are locked, I suck down another drink of my soda then get out of the car. Maybe Lucas told her I was coming and she left the door unlocked for me?

No such luck. The front is, of course, secured. Growing up at Grandma Dot's farm, we never locked the doors. She still rarely locks them. But this is a far cry from the secure farm where Grandma Dot lives. Dustin grumbles at Grandma for her lack of security. There's no way he'd let his own house go unlocked.

Since Alexis's window is on the right, I go left around the house. The lighted displays of the neighbor's are all in the front yards. As I enter the backyard, I'm plunged into relative darkness. The patio door glows in the dim. Sheer curtains provide privacy, but the lighted tree inside makes them glow.

I push on the sliding door, but it's locked, too. Cupping my hands around my face, I look inside to get an idea of the layout. As I remember, this part of the house is basically one big room. Kitchen, dining and living room all open. Mostly, I'm hoping Olivia isn't sleeping on the couch, leaving me no options.

Through the sheers, I can't make out

details, but the hulking L-shaped couch in the center of the room doesn't have a girl-shaped blob on it.

I push on the sliding door again, hoping it was just frozen shut, not locked. It slides a fraction of an inch, then catches. The small movement is encouraging, I will get in, somehow.

I hurry back to my car and dig a credit card out of my purse. The card has been maxed out for two months, ever since I lost my job. At least now it can serve a purpose. I pull the two filled present bags along with me, sliding them through the snow. With the bags lugging behind me, I feel like the Grinch dragging all the toys away from Whoville. At least I'm dragging the toys the opposite direction.

Opening the sliding door with the credit card is unsettlingly easy. I once watched a few YouTube videos on lock-picking when I was killing time at the shop, but I'm by far not an expert. If I can break in after a few jiggles of my maxed out Visa, Dustin needs to invest in a new lock.

For now, I'm happy it was easy.

I slide the door open. The door slides easily, but the faint scratching sound makes me cringe. I stick my head inside the door and the soft fabric of the sheer curtain clings to my curls. I pull it away, and the combination of my gloves, my hair and the curtain causes a flurry of static electricity snaps. Charged now, the curtain again clings to my hair. Swiping at the stupid fabric, I step inside onto the tiled entrance.

A sound and a movement on the far side of the room near the hall makes me duck low, hidden behind the couch. The sound is rhythmic, not threatening. I raise myself enough to see over the couch. On a table near the hall, an elf with an oversized red hat climbs a ladder up a tree, slides down, and climbs again. I imagine Walker gets a kick out of it, but the climbing elf got my heart pumping.

"Get a grip, kid," I say to myself, then return to my mission.

Feeling both naughty for breaking in and nice for bringing the presents in the first place,

I shove the door open and drag the bags inside. The crinkle of the plastic bags seems to fill the quiet house, setting my nerves on edge. The first bag comes through no problem, but one of the boxes in the second bag is wide and catches on the door. "Stupid box."

I bend over to turn the box so it will fit.

Something crashes to the tile under my boots. A loud hiss mixes with the sound of my startled cry. The second soda can from Lucas's explodes, spraying dark liquid in all directions, spinning and squirting sticky streaks on the white sheers and pale carpet.

"Stop, stop," I whisper to the spinning can, watching helplessly as the mess grows. My tired brain finally catches on to what happened. I grab the can and toss it out the door onto the patio. It continues to hiss and sizzle, but the snow doesn't care if it gets sticky.

I look at the mess with a sinking feeling. Cherry Pepsi pools in the grout lines of the tile, a pool of it near the edge, where it poured onto the carpet. Dark liquid looks like blood spatter on the white curtains. Soda pours off the plastic bags when I move them.

"Crap on a cracker," I whisper. "What a mess."

The quiet of the house is suddenly shattered.

"Freeze. I have a gun."

I've never heard Alexis's voice so firm and in control. I'm actually impressed by her. Crouched by the patio door with my back to her and the couch between us, it's no wonder she thinks I'm a burglar.

I put my hands up just to be safe. Standing slowly, I turn around. "It's just me, Alexis," I say in the most soothing voice I can manage facing the business end of a gun.

Alexis doesn't drop the small pistol, keeps it pointed at my chest. A horrible thought jumps through my head. Alexis has never liked me. She could easily shoot me now, and claim she thought I was a robber. I did break in, after all.

She doesn't hate you that much.

The gun doesn't move.

Does she?

"Alexis, put down the gun. It's just Gabby," I say.

"Gabby?" She lowers the gun a few inches, but still holds it ready to use. "Why are you breaking into my house?"

With my hands still in the air and a gun still pointed in my direction, my patience is slipping. "You know, I would love to tell you all about it, but you have to put the gun away first, okay?"

She looks at the gun in her hand, seems surprised to see it. She drops it on the table near the climbing elf. "I, uh." The firm, impressive voice she used a few moments ago is gone. She runs both hands into her hair, pushes against her temples, squeezes her eyes shut as if in pain. "Jesus, Gabby. I'm so sorry. I had a migraine earlier and took an extra sleeping pill."

My irritation switches to concern. I've never seen Alexis like this. She always seems so put together, so in control. Every hair in place, not a stain on any shirt she wears.

"I'm sorry I scared you. Obviously, Lucas

didn't tell you I was bringing over Olivia's gifts."

Alexis shakes her head hard. I'm not sure if she's saying no to me, or just trying to shake the pain out. "I didn't know, but I guess I should have assumed something like that before I pulled a gun on you." She tries to make a chuckle, but it comes out as a half-sob. "Some Christmas, huh?"

"Most Christmases are kind of a mess for me." I shrug, keeping the massive couch between us just in case.

Alexis walks into the kitchen part of the room and gets herself a glass of water. "Better get used to ruined Christmases if you plan on marrying a cop," she says, then downs the whole glass of water in one long drink.

This is another side of Alexis I've never seen. I let the marrying comment slide. Lucas and I haven't gotten anywhere near that discussion yet, but I feel certain we will someday.

"Ruined birthday parties," Alexis continues. "Ruined weekend plans. Even a nice dinner out together rarely happens without some kind of police work messing it up."

I don't know how to respond to any of this. I'm not even certain she realizes she's talking to me. Some of those sleeping pills can mess your mind up pretty bad. I let her ramble, and focus on my immediate problem.

"Can I get some wet rags and some towels?" I ask her. "I kind of made a mess over here."

Alexis snaps out of her sad funk, and gathers up the cleaning supplies.

"What in the world did you do?" she asks once she sees the spill.

"Dropped a soda can and it exploded."

With stiff movements and an exasperated attitude, she helps me clean the floor. This is the Alexis I know. In control and annoyed with me.

"I'll have to wash the curtains tomorrow," she grumbles as she gathers up the wet towels and takes them into the kitchen and out of sight towards the laundry room.

While she's gone, I place Olivia's gifts

under the tree, thankful to finally have the seemingly simple task completed. I notice a few of the boxes have tags with my name on them. I fight the urge to shake them, or even touch them too much. I want to be surprised.

My task complete and my mess cleaned up, I crumple up the bags inside out so nothing sticky is exposed. Alexis has been gone a long time. I awkwardly wait near the tree with the wad of bags in my hands. I watch the elf climb the ladder five times before my concern and curiosity get the better of me.

"Alexis?" I walk into the kitchen. "I'm all done."

Down a short hall, the laundry room light is on, and I can hear the washer filling, but Alexis doesn't answer.

"Hello?" I call gently, wondering where she went. The door to the garage is in front of me, but I didn't hear her open it. That leaves only the laundry room.

Confused, I peak around the corner of the door jamb. The small room barely has space for the washer and dryer, let alone the

92

overflowing baskets of clothes on the floor. I find her on top of the baskets, curled on her side in the laundry and fast asleep.

I shake her shoulder, but she doesn't wake up. The faint, but unmistakable scent of wine wafts from her. "Migraine medicine, sleeping pills and wine?" I ask. "No wonder you're acting so strange."

Shaking doesn't wake her completely, but I manage to rouse her enough to get her to her feet. Leaning heavily against me, she lets me lead her down the hall to her bed. The electric candle in the window shines through the drapes. It bathes the room in a comforting red glow, but I imagine it does nothing to fill Dustin's absence.

Alexis topples into the bed, her hands searching the empty space next to her. She finds the largest pillow and wraps her arms around the red checked poof. I'm familiar with the move. In my own bed, I wrap around Chester, but the reason is the same. Sleeping alone sucks.

Once she's settled and comfortable, I leave

her to her sad dreams, wondering if in the morning, she'll remember I was here at all.

The door directly across the hall is open a few inches. Walker's room. I peak through the crack of the door. Walker is asleep in his crib, laying face down, but on his knees so his butt is in the air. Olivia sleeps on the floor next to him, on a pile of blankets and cushions. The moonlight filters through the curtains and I can just make out her features. She reminds me so much of her dad, it makes me smile.

If you're going to marry a cop.

If I marry Lucas, this little girl will be my daughter. The thought makes my smile grow larger. Olivia and I don't know each other very well yet, but I care about her a lot already.

"Merry Christmas, Olivia," I whisper through the crack in the door.

Back in the living room, I remember the gun. Alexis sat in on the table next to the climbing elf. The table has other bright decorations on it and a nativity set complete with a small wooden barn.

The black gun, so close to Baby Jesus,

makes me sick to my stomach. I snatch the gun off the table, whispering, "Sorry, Jesus. She didn't mean it."

Dustin would be furious if he knew Alexis not only pulled a gun on me, but then left it out and loaded with the kids in the house. I try to think of a place to hide it. I could put it in a cabinet or in the garage or something, but Dustin might stumble across it. He'd then grill Alexis about it. I've been on the receiving end of many of his lectures. Saving Alexis from one is my Christmas gift to her.

She's obviously going through something and I don't trust her with it right now. That's a discussion for later. For now, I just need to keep the gun safe. Not knowing what else to do with it, I check to make sure the safety is on, then shove it into my coat pocket.

Despite all the excitement of the night and the caffeine I've been drinking, I stifle a yawn. With the gun heavy in my pocket I lock the patio door and let myself out the front door, locking it behind me. The plastic wreath bumps gently against the door as it closes.

My gloves are sticky and wet from the exploded soda, so I pull them off. With bare fingers, I touch the trailing end of the huge red bow.

A shimmer of Mom in happier times flits through my head. I welcome the image, hungry for any scrap of my mother.

I wrap my fingers around the ribbon, and the vision shifts. Dustin in Grandma Dot's attic. The sling on his arm tells me the vision is recent.

Sorry I doubted you, guilt and shame, a dash of hope, tears and pain.

I let go of the ribbon, embarrassed to see Dustin in such a private moment. I normally don't get visions from those closest to me. I've never *seen* Dustin.

My tattoo tingles gently, pleasantly.

I look to the sky. "Thank you," I say to God. Getting to know my brother better, actually seeing him, is a precious gift.

Thinking of Dustin brings me back to the reason he's not here.

I'm super curious what Lucas and Dustin

have found out about the missing kids and want to help in the search. Back in my Charger, I unload Alexis's gun, check the safety just to be sure and put the whole mess in my glove box. My glove box is actually used as a "glove box." A collection of random gloves tumbles onto the floor in a rainbow of fabric.

"Crap on a cracker." I gather as many of the loose gloves as possible and shove them around the gun. I slam the little door closed before more gloves can fall out. I toss my wet and sticky gloves onto the passenger seat, and pick a different pair from the floor. I usually stock up on black or gray gloves, neutral colors. My favorites are tan ones that blend in with my skin, so people don't stare. The gloves on the floor are all bright colored ones, the reason they're shoved away in the first place.

Grandma Dot loves buying me what she calls *fun gloves*. "Embrace it, Gabriella. Show off your sassy," she'd say. I have no idea what that means, but I know there will be at least one present tomorrow morning that is brightly colored gloves. As a nod to Grandma and the holiday, I choose the most garish of the selection on my floor board. One has a red hand with each finger a different color, the other is dark blue with hot pink stripes. I hold my hands up to take a look.

"Goes with the ridiculous hoodie you're wearing," I say to myself with an over-tired giggle.

Before I put the car in drive with my blue and pink hand, I text Lucas, "Santa duty is done. What next?"

While I wait for his response, I drive slowly through the quiet, well-lit neighborhood and sip on the last of the soda.

"Nothing you can do tonight. LUVU."

The short-hand 'love you' takes the sting out of the dismissal. Another yawn makes my jaw ache. Lucas and Dustin may be used to working all night, but I'm used to regular sleep and lots of it.

At the exit of the housing addition, I can't decide which way to turn. Left would take me back towards town, my empty bed and fitful night of worry. Right takes me towards Grandma Dot's. The bed will still be empty and my mind will still be full of worry, but at least Grandma will be there.

And Mom.

A few weeks ago, my mom, Emily McAllister, was cleared of all charges and released from prison. After fifteen years of her not being here, I'm still getting used to her return.

The decision easily made, I turn right and head towards Grandma Dot's farm.

Chapter 7

LUCAS

Dustin takes the front seat of the cruiser, so I'm forced to sit in back. The seat is hard and uncomfortable and something gooey makes my pants stick to the seat. Tonight I don't care. The death of Lauren Whitlow has sucker punched all other concerns from my mind.

She shouldn't have died. She seemed hurt, but stable, recoverable.

I missed something, should have done something.

On the drive back to the police department, the dark fields and farm houses slide past my eyes. For once, I don't drink in the details the way I've been trained. Outside is just a dark blur. Dustin and Patterson, the officer driving us, chat, but their words flow past me like a soft breeze. The only words I can hear are repeating in my head.

You could have saved her.

I pinch the bridge of my nose, irritated with myself. Rationally, I know there wasn't anything I could have done differently. If Gabby hadn't sensed them and if I hadn't seen the tracks before the rising storm obliterated them, she would still be sitting in the wrecked car, growing cold, her family having no idea where she was. Or where Eric Landry was.

"You said the male victim was Eric Landry," I interrupt Dustin and Patterson. "What do we know about him?"

Dustin turns as well as he can with his injured arm to face me. "Driver's license says he lives on Anders Street. Previously married to Bethany Landry. No children."

"What about Lauren Whitlow? What's her story?"

"Lives out in Crestwood. Married to Jared Whitlow. My guess is her marriage is still legal, but on paper only and Landry was the new man. Doesn't seem like she'd have her kids with her secret affair on Christmas Eve, but who knows."

"Any luck on finding the car that picked the kids up?" I already know the answer to this question, but maybe some detail came over the radio while I wasn't paying attention. I can hope.

Dustin shakes his head and turns back to face the front of the car. "Not much to go on. You didn't see it?"

"By the time I got there, it was already gone." I won't tell him how I found Gabby crawling and desperate. Dustin won't understand and Patterson doesn't need to hear it.

"Pretty amazing how Gabby knew to look for them," Patterson surprises me with the praise. He'd seen Gabby's work up close the night Dustin was shot. She must have made an impression on him. Thank God it was a good impression, many of the other officers don't share his opinion.

"She can do some amazing stuff," I say proudly. I sense Dustin tense up, but he keeps his mouth shut.

"Can't she just touch one of the kid's toys and sense where they are, or something like that?" Patterson pushes.

Dustin coughs, a badly executed attempt to hide his derision. If I could reach him through the divider on the cruiser, I'd smack him in the back of the head.

"It doesn't work like that, exactly," I explain.

"Too bad," Patterson continues, oblivious to Dustin's reactions. "Would sure make our work a lot easier."

Dustin coughs again, but it can't cover his scoff. "Trust me," he says. "Working with Gabby has its challenges."

"And it's benefits," I jump in. "Even you have to admit she's a big help."

Patterson looks at Dustin, then over his shoulder at me, confused by the rising tension in the car. "Either way, I like her." Patterson attempts to divert the situation. "Where are you detectives headed after you get changed and in your own car? Her family first, or his?"

"Hers," Dustin says with finality.

"Hopefully the estranged husband has the kids, and everything is just fine."

"He doesn't have a four door light colored sedan registered to him," I point out. "Just a Tahoe."

"Maybe we'll still get lucky," Dustin says tiredly, rubbing the shoulder in a sling. A few minutes ago, I had the urge to smack him, now I worry. The section of his face I can see is tight and drawn with pain, his skin pale.

"You know you're not officially back to work yet," I point out. "This isn't actually your case. You should sit this one out."

Dustin snaps his head around in defense. "I'm not sitting this out. Not until we know the kids are safe. That could be Walker or Olivia out there."

I knew mentioning stepping aside would rile him up, which is why I said it. Color returns to his cheeks and his eyes snap. "As long as you're up for it," I say, the corner of my mouth twitching.

Dustin sees the twitch, realizes I was playing him. "I don't know what my sister sees in you," he says shuffling back around to face forward. "You're lucky there's a divider between us. I could take you with just my one arm."

We pull into the parking garage and I blink against the sudden brightness of the overhead lights. "Once I get out of this car, there won't be a divider to keep you safe," I tease back.

"Detectives are odd," Patterson says good-naturedly, and parks the car. "Get out. I'm not an Uber driver." He smiles at me through the rearview mirror, joining in.

Dustin climbs out and starts walking away, knowing full well I can't open my door from the inside.

"Hey," I yell, banging on the door.

He looks over his shoulder and laughs, but waits for me at the doors.

Patterson gets out and opens the door for me. "Like I said, detectives are weird."

I clamp Patterson on the shoulder in a friendly gesture. "That's how we stay sane."

"I get that. Whatever it takes." His face grows serious and he hooks one thumb into his belt taking a nervous posture. "Good luck tonight. I don't envy you."

"Worst part of the job," I say seriously, looking across the bright parking garage and rubbing my hand down my face. "It's hard to destroy a family then be forced to watch the fall out."

"You didn't destroy these families," Patterson says. "Whoever forced them off the road did."

"Thanks man," I say sincerely. "I needed that." I put out my hand to shake his. I don't know the rookie well, but I like what I've seen. He grips my hand, firm, but not too hard. "Thanks for the ride."

"Merry Christmas, Detective Hartley." He releases my hand. "Tell Gabby thank you for her help tonight."

Warmed by Patterson thinking of Gabby, I say, "I'll give you a good review on the Uber app."

He waves his hand in dismissal at my levity as he climbs back into the cruiser to return to patrol.

Dustin is waiting for me at the double glass doors that enter the station. "I wouldn't give him more than three stars," he says. "Dirty car. You should see the stain on your pants from the back seat."

I crane my neck to see whatever had me stuck to the seat, try to catch a reflection from the glass doors. The stain is out of view. "I don't want to know. I'll probably have to burn these pants now."

"Don't worry, fashion diva, you look better in uniform anyway." Dustin pushes through the doors and into the station.

Changed into my uniform, and dressed for action, I feel like a different man. My mind skitters over Olivia and Gabby. I'm certain Olivia is safe with Alexis. I'm just as certain Gabby will make sure to take the gifts over for the morning. I'm not used to having a helper. Not used to trusting another person to take care of something like that for me.

God bless that woman.

I need to think about another woman now, Lauren Whitlow. I shut my locker and the dark blue door rattles. "Ready?" I ask Dustin. His color is a little better and I saw him take a pain pill as we changed, but he's struggling now. His foot is propped up on the wooden bench between the rows of lockers, and he's trying to tie his boot with his one good hand. "Here, let me," I offer.

Dustin reluctantly allows me to tie his boots, staring awkwardly past my shoulders. "Don't you dare say a thing," he warns. "Or I'll kick you with this boot."

I instinctively draw my knees together, but don't expect a kick. We may joke around, but I know where to draw the line. Either of us would take a bullet for the other, tying his boots is nothing. "Shut up and let's go."

This late at night, River Bend feels like it's sleeping, waiting for morning and the wonder of Christmas. Only a few cars pass us as we drive through town towards the addition of Crestwood listed as Laruen Whitlow's last address. None of the cars are light colored, four door sedans, which, in itself, shows how few cars are out.

The Crestwood housing addition rarely gets police traffic. The residents are mostly executives with jobs in Fort Wayne that they commute to or other professional types. The neighborhood consists of about twenty large lots of an acre or so each. Large houses grace the carefully manicured lots, many with extra detached buildings. Each house was designed to resemble a mixture of late-Victorian and modern architecture. Tall windows, round turrets, wide porches and plenty of gingerbread accents grace each home. Outbuildings that look like carriage houses, elaborate play houses, or even wrought iron greenhouses, dot many of the yards.

"I always loved this neighborhood," I tell Dustin. "The old style of homes was so pretty. Add in a big kitchen and walk-in closets, and I'm sold."

"Keep dreaming," he says. "Not on our salary."

Even the light displays are tastefully done. If we were here for another reason, I'd enjoy the drive. Maybe I'll bring Gabby out here sometime just to walk around.

"Look at that play house," I point to one of the back yards. "It actually looks like a ship. Wouldn't Walker love that?"

"That princess castle is two stories high," Dustin says with amazement, anxiously jumping at any topic other than the one that brings us here in the middle of the night.

"Olivia would go nuts." I am so enthralled by the playhouses, I miss the address listed for Lauren Whitlow. I stop on the road and back up. Her house is across the street from the princess castle house.

Once I pull into the drive and turn off the lights, Dustin and I take a moment to collect ourselves. We've been joking around all night, avoiding the obvious out of self-protection. Now we're here. If Jared Whitlow still lives here, he either has the kids with him and the whole case will be wrapped up soon, or we're about to ruin his life.

If he's not here, we have a whole other problem.

Either outcome isn't good.

An animated group of white-lighted deer lift and lower their heads in the front yard. A tree that fills the entire front window of the house pours light onto the porch. A tree that would have been full of gifts in the morning.

"Maybe no one's home," Dustin says. "It's likely the husband moved out. This is listed as his address, but maybe he didn't change it yet."

"Or maybe Eric Landry was just a family friend and the Whitlows were happily married."

Even as I say the words, I don't believe them. If Jared Whitlow's wife and kids were out with a friend and not back by now, he would have called it in. Or at least be up pacing the floors.

Besides the movement of the deer decorations, the house is still. From the driveway, we can't see any lights on inside besides the Christmas tree.

We have to try, anyway.

Ice crunches under our boots on the steps up the front porch. Lovely, fresh cut pine swags hang from the front porch railing, the scent of the wood drifting on the breeze. Before we knock, we look through the large front window dominated by the tree. I can see past the tree, through the living room and into the kitchen in back. "I got nothing."

At the far end of the porch, a rounded section of the house juts out, then reaches three stories high. Dustin cups his face and looks inside.

"Some kind of office, maybe," he says. "No one inside."

The front door is double wide. Each side is dark wood with cut glass windows. A massive wreath of fresh pine adorns one of the doors. Using the back end of my flashlight, I bang on the other door. If anyone is home, they will hear it.

A dog barks from inside, the high-pitched yip frantic and insistent.

I knock again, louder.

The dog goes crazy, scratching and clawing at the wooden front door. Growling and yapping like it wants to tear our socks off if he can just get to our ankles.

"Cujo," Dustin jokes.

"Thinks he is, at least."

One more knock, just to be sure.

"Pickles, stop it," a mumbled voice says from behind the door.

Dustin and I exchange surprised looks. Someone is home after all, but it's not Jared Whitlow.

"Be quiet you dumb dog," the woman says. "Who's out there?" she asks loudly. "It's late, what do you want?"

"Detectives McAllister and Hartley with the River Bend Police Department," Dustin says, holding his badge near the glass window in the center of the door. "Is this the home of Lauren Whitlow?"

"Oh my God," the woman wails. The dog makes a sudden squeal of pain and I imagine the woman kicked it out of the way. "What's happened?" She fumbles with the lock and the handle. "Pickles, get away!"

"Can we come in?" I ask as gently as possible.

With a final rattle of the handle, the door

flies open. "What happened to my daughter?" The woman demands.

Chapter 8

LUCAS

The look of terrified expectation on the woman's face is an expression I'm familiar with. A police officer at your door at any time of day is cause for alarm. A late at night visit by detectives when your loved ones aren't home is a nightmare come true. I want to sink into the porch, to slink away like the harbinger of horror that I am. I want to say, "Your daughter is fine. We're just going door-to-door to wish everyone a Merry Christmas." I want to be home in bed, Gabby curled next to me, Olivia in the next room dreaming of Santa.

I swore an oath, and this is part of it.

"May we come in, ma'am?" Dustin asks softly.

Lauren Whitlow's mother wraps her thick robe tighter around her, shrinking into the white fabric sprinkled with red snowflakes. She clings to the opening under her chin as if closing her robe completely can protect her from what's coming.

"Come in." She backs away from the door, away from Dustin and me. Her eyes are wide and fixed on us as if we are killers in a slasher movie. She looks ready to turn and run.

"I'm so sorry we are here," I say, holding my hands up in an open, non-threatening gesture. "Are you Lauren Whitlow's mother?

She nods, but keeps backing up until she runs into the wall on the far side of the front room. Startled, she makes a small sound of pain. Pickles the dog, thankfully has stopped barking and cowers behind her legs, peeking his fluffy white face out now and then from the hem of the red snowflake robe. "I'm Teresa. I came to visit Lauren and the kids for the holiday." She works the robe under her chin, squeezing and releasing the fuzzy fabric. "Where are they?" Teresa looks wildly around the room, searching for the clock. "It's really late. Lauren and the kids should have been home by now. Ian and Cora's bed time was hours ago. Oliver would of course beg to stay up. Lauren probably will let him, but Ian and Cora…."

"Teresa," I say gently, placing a hand on her elbow and leading her to an oversized loveseat near the expertly decorated tree. "Please sit down." She lets me guide her to the chair and sinks into the deep blue cushions. She pulls the decorative pillow with a reindeer embroidered on it from behind her back and holds it to her chest. Pickles jumps onto her lap, his body shaking against the pillow. The lights of the tree fall across her terrified face, reflect on the tears swelling in her eyes.

I don't dance around the issue. I've found being direct and clear is the best way to deliver the blow. Like tearing off the largest band-aid in the world, I tell her the news quickly.

Dustin and I turn our eyes away out of respect as Teresa absorbs the initial shock and crumples. I struggle to keep up my professional armor, my professional detachment. I search for something to focus my eyes on while we wait for Teresa. The massive Christmas tree dominates the room. A few presents are under the tree already, each one tagged with "From Grams." The presents waiting for the missing children burns my heart and spurs me to be a bit more blunt than I normally would.

"Teresa," I interrupt her sobs. "I know this is difficult, but we need to ask you a few questions."

She blinks rapidly and wipes her face on the collar of her robe, leaving a smear on one of the red snowflakes. "I'll do the best I can," she says bravely.

"What can you tell us about Lauren and Jared's marriage?" Dustin asks. "She and the kids were in the car with a different man."

Dustin made the statement as neutral as possible, but Teresa takes offense.

"Lauren was not having an affair, if that's what you're trying to insinuate." She sits up straighter and a more natural color returns to her face. "Lauren and Jared have been separated for nearly a year now. They are only married on paper at this point, and that was going to be final next week. The *other man* was Eric." Her voice catches on his name, realizing afresh that he has passed, too. "Eric and Lauren have been dating for several months. He's a good man. Nothing scandalous was happening." Teresa lifts her chin, daring us to defy her.

"We weren't insinuating anything like that," I assure her. "With the kids in the car, we didn't think Lauren was sneaking around."

Teresa nods, one firm dip of her head.

"Back to Jared Whitlow," Dustin says. "This is listed as his address. He obviously doesn't live here, so do you know where we can find him?"

Teresa practically bounces in her seat with hope. "Do you think he has the kids? He wouldn't hurt them, so they could be safe at his house right now, sound asleep."

Dustin does his best to quench her growing hope, "The children were picked up by a light colored four door sedan. Jared doesn't own one does he?"

"I don't think so. He's been driving the truck, and Lauren drives the red car. How do you know the kids were taken in a different car?"

Dustin looks at me, and I answer for him. "A consultant on the case saw them climb into the car. She was too far away to make out more than the vague description. She did say the kids went willingly and didn't seem to be in distress."

Teresa thinks on the information. "I don't know who that might have been, but then again, I'm just visiting. I live in Louisville and only come up here once or twice a year. Normally, Lauren and the kids come to me for the holidays. She's so proud of this house, she wanted to spend Christmas here. They just moved in here in January. Wasn't long after that, she and Jared started having problems." She absently pets Pickles, and mutters, "If she'd come to me, none of this would have happened."

Fresh tears slide down her cheeks, drip off her chin and fall on the dog. She makes no move to wipe them away, and Pickles doesn't notice.

Dustin prods gently, "Do you have an address for Jared? Or his phone number?"

Teresa answers, emptily. "He moved to the Autumn Hills Apartments. I don't know which apartment, but Oliver said their back patio is close to the park. Said it was the only good thing about the place."

Dustin steps into the next room to call the information in so Jared Whitlow can be located.

While he's gone, Teresa scrubs at the tears and rubs her face hard. "Oliver is such a good boy. He's just turned nine. Cora's only five, but she acts like she's Ian's mommy. Please find them. Please find my grandkids." The raw emotion on her face, etches another scar into my memories of faces I've changed with my life shattering news.

"We are doing everything we can," I assure her, patting her hand. Pickles growls low in his throat, warning me to stay back. "Is there anyone who you can call to come stay with you tonight? You shouldn't be alone right now."

Teresa shakes her head. "My husband died a few years ago. My friends and most of our family are in Louisville. Lauren's brother is there, and my sister." She pulls the pillow tighter against her chest, her words begin spinning out. "Oh my, I have to tell them what happened. And it's Christmas. Oh Lord. I can't do that to them, but they have to know." Her eyes dart around the room as if looking for her family.

"The calls can wait," I interrupt her, pulling her back to the conversation. "At least until morning. There's no one in River Bend that you are close to?"

Her eyes fall on a table near the front door. "Not really. I know Jared's mom, Paula, pretty well. She's been friendly with Lauren through the divorce. She even brought that tray of cookies over earlier this evening, right before Lauren left." Teresa crushes the pillow under her chin. "I can't be the one to tell her the kids are missing. I just can't. Have you told Jared yet?"

Dustin returns to the couch. "We have officers at his apartment right now looking for him."

"Right, right," Teresa mumbles. "Of course."

"Where were Lauren and Eric and the kids tonight? Did they go to a party or something?" asks Dustin.

"The kids weren't here. They were spending the night at their dad's. Lauren wasn't happy about it, but she wanted to keep the peace, you know. The divorce was almost final and she didn't want to rock the boat. Plus, the kids would be home in the morning and we'd have the whole day together."

"So how did the kids get in the car?" Dustin asks.

"Lauren and Eric were going to spend the evening at a friend's, but right before they left, Jared called. I didn't hear the actual conversation, but I could tell by Lauren's tone that something was wrong. When she hung up, she was upset, and gloating a little bit, if I'm honest. She said to me, 'Told you he couldn't handle it on his own.' She and Eric left soon after that. I assumed to pick the kids up from Jared's, but I didn't ask any questions.

"Jared was supposed to have the kids all night?"

Teresa nods and pulls Pickles close to her chest. "They should never have been in the car with Lauren and Eric. They should be safe at their dad's right now, not out with God knows who." Her voice breaks on the last note. Pickles squirms against her too tight grip, and she lets him go.

"We'll find them, Teresa. They went willingly into the car, just focus on that. If they know their abductor, the odds are good they aren't being hurt." I hope she believes the line. Truth is, nothing about a child abduction is normal.

The word abductor makes her flinch and tears stream quietly again. Straining to hold herself together, she asks, "Do you need anything else from me right now? I'd very much like to be alone."

Dustin and I get to our feet, taking the hint. Dustin gives her a card along with the line about calling if she needs anything or thinks of anything that can be helpful to the investigation.

The word investigation makes her flinch again. Dustin sees the flinch, and his face pales another shade. "Are you sure you don't want to call anyone to come be with you tonight?" he asks.

Teresa clenches the robe closed under her chin again. "Honestly, Detective, I just want to take a Benadryl, crawl back into bed and pretend none of this is real. Tomorrow, I'll call my son and my sister and I'm sure they will be here by afternoon. For now, I want them to enjoy the holiday. There's nothing to be gained telling them the horrible news now."

She holds her back stiff, as if relaxing at all will cause her to crumble to the floor. Dustin and I hesitate at the door, ready to let ourselves out. "You are quite a woman, Teresa." The words pop out of my mouth before I realize

I'm going to say them. "Lauren and your son are lucky to have had you as a mother."

Maybe it's the recent betrayal of my own mom, or the quiet dignity of the mother standing before me, but my professional code breaks. I pull the woman into my arms, and she slumps against my vest. Her entire body shakes, her control slipping away. Her sobs are heavy and deep, each one cutting into my heart.

I can't imagine her pain, don't want to imagine it. All I can do is hold her and make this moment, right here, a little better.

Dustin politely looks away, pretends to be interested in the decorations on the table near the door and the plate of cookies brought by another woman whose grandchildren are missing. He rubs at his shoulder, digs out another pill from his pocket and dry swallows it.

After a few minutes, Teresa pulls away, wiping her red and blotchy face with the collar of her robe. The ram-rod tension of her body is a little looser. "Sorry, about that," she says nervously, backing away.

Dustin saves me from having to answer, from acknowledging my lapse in decorum. "We'll be in touch as soon as we know anything." He flicks his eyes at me, then opens the front door and steps onto the porch.

"Thank you, Detective," she says in a voice so low, only I can hear. "I really needed that." She makes a strangled sound that's half way between a laugh and a squeal. Flustered, she latches onto her deeply ingrained manners. "Here, take one of these cookies," she hands me the treat, her fingers shaking, then makes the odd half laugh sound again.

"Thank you," I say genuinely, pulling one of my own cards from my shirt pocket. "This is my card. If you need something, even if it's not about the case, just call me, okay."

She takes the card and presses it to her chest. "I will."

"I hate leaving you here alone. Promise you'll be safe, and call me if you need to talk, or to whatever."

She nods soberly, understanding the

meaning under my words. "Don't worry, Detective Hartley. As I said, my son and my sister will surely come tomorrow. I won't be alone." She picks up Pickles, his fluffy white curls blending into the white and red pattern of her robe.

I hear Dustin shuffling on the front porch and cold air is pouring in through the open door. "You watch after her," I say to Pickles. "Take good care of her." I'm not sure why I'm stalling. We have a mountain of work to do tonight to find the missing kids. Dustin clears his throat and I take the hint.

I move my hand from Pickles to her shoulder and give it a pat. "Merry Christmas, Teresa," I say quietly. I turn on my heel and step onto the porch. Teresa shuts the door behind me.

The click of the latch and the lock are loud in the deep quiet of the snow covered night. Our boots crunch in the snow as we walk back to the cruiser.

"She didn't give me a cookie." Dustin makes an attempt to lighten the mood.

I take the bait thankfully. "Guess she likes me better." I put the cookie to my lips ready to take a bite.

Justin Timberlake singing "I'm Bringing Sexy Back" cuts into the quiet night. Startled by the sound of my phone, I drop the cookie into the snow and fumble in my pocket to turn off the racy song.

"Good thing that didn't go off in her house," Dustin points out, a massive grin on his face. "Let me guess, my sister?"

I finally manage to pull the phone from my pocket and stop the song from playing. "She set that as her text tone the other day. I don't know how to change it."

"Sure you don't," Dustin teases and sings a few lines of the song as he walks around the car to the passenger side. He suddenly grows serious, "She okay?"

The message from Gabby is short. "Santa duty is done. What next?"

"She's fine. She just finished dropping off Olivia's gifts at your house and wants to know what else she can do."

Dustin continues singing the Justin Timberlake song and climbs into the car without a comment about Gabby. I wonder if the pill he just took is responsible for his happy mood. Considering what we've been doing for the last hour, it's the only explanation.

I text a response to Gabby, "Nothing you can do tonight. LUVU," and then climb into the cruiser. "What now?"

"We need to find Jared Whitlow."

"Autumn Hills Apartments." I put the cruiser into gear and drive out of the lovely, Victorian-inspired neighborhood. Earlier, I'd wanted to bring Gabby here to walk around or go for a run. Looking at all the beautiful homes, I wish I could buy one of them for her. For a few glorious moments, I imagine a life here with Gabby and Olivia.

Dustin's radio crackles and the imaginary life disappears.

"They've located Jared Whitlow," he says. "He does not have the kids."

"He may not have them, but maybe he knows who does."

I speed through the last block of the wonderful neighborhood and turn onto the main road. The sparkling, holiday lights of the estates fade in my rear view mirror. The faint hope of the children being found safe and sound with their dad fades too, replaced with a feeling of dread.

Chapter 9

GABBY

The blasting snow storm from earlier has settled into an eerie quiet. The homes and farms I pass sleep under the blanket of clouds. The full moon behind the cloud makes the entire sky glow with a soft light. On the country roads returning me to Grandma's farm, the Christmas lights are fewer, mostly just the occasional strand tacked around a window, or a net of lights tossed on a bush.

Except for the Gottlieb Estate. The owners not only gave their home a pretentious name, complete with a large sign and a wrought iron fence, they also have a massive light display. They no doubt paid a professional to hang the lights. I can't imagine the owners of a place like this dragging out their ladders and boxes of lights. I can't imagine them doing any of the work a place like this requires themselves. I'm sure they have a landscaper take care of the wide lawn and the well tended trees growing inside the fence.

"They probably even have a maid to do the cleaning and a cook to make dinner," I complain. My stomach grumbles in response. Grandma Dot's lovely dinner was hours ago and the few tootsie rolls I found on the floorboard while picking up my gloves did little except make my teeth hurt.

Despite my jealousy thinly disguised as loathing, I find myself slowing to take in the show. The money was well spent as the display is spectacular. My Charger crawls along the black iron fence and drifts to a stop.

My tattoo tingles, just a bit, but enough for me to put the car in park and take a closer look at the Gottlieb Estate. From my car, I don't see anything amiss. Besides the holiday lights, the house is dark inside. I step out into the snow and walk along the fence. The gate is locked, of course, but I can still look.

Not sure what I'm looking for, I drag my

hand along the bars, the different colored fingers of my glove ticking from bar to bar, like a convict killing time. I don't see anything my tattoo should be interested in.

Once I reach the end of the fence, I turn the corner and follow it down the side of the property. My heart starts to race. Walking along the roadside is one thing, but the side of the property is another. Either I'm trespassing on any land the Gottliebs own outside of the fence, or I'm intruding on the neighboring property. I don't worry too much about the owner of the open field caring about my presence, but the Gottliebs, whoever they are, probably won't be pleased to see me stalking their fence.

The expansive home has a side entrance garage so large I could fit four of my houses in it. The concrete parking area is flat and smooth, not a crack in sight. An entire fleet of cars could park outside of the massive garage.

In fact, only one car is parked outside.

My trek along the fence comes to an abrupt halt. The car looks familiar. A light colored four door sedan, it isn't remarkable by itself, but the sticker in the window is. The shape is familiar, so is its placement.

I need to get closer to see the sticker, make sure this car isn't the one that took the kids. I grab a bar in each hand and try to haul myself up. My cotton gloves just slide down the bars. Frustrated, I yank off the gloves and try again. The icy bars sting my sensitive palms, but no matter how hard I grip, I can't climb over.

Blowing warm air onto my fingers first, I wrap my bare left hand on a bar and open my mind. I listen hard for the children, for the kidnapper, for anything to guide me.

The cold metal stings my hand, but nothing else happens.

Discouraged, I put the bright gloves back on and search for a way onto the estate. I follow the fence all the way around back and down the other side. Besides an expensive looking outdoor "kitchen" on the huge patio, the backyard is like all other yards tonight – buried in snow. I eventually make the entire trek back to my car. I can't leave without touching the car, or maybe even looking into some of the dark windows of the house. I need to be sure the kids aren't here.

The kidnapped kids could be behind this fence. It's a perfect place to hide. No one can get in or out without the code to the gate. No one would imagine the Gottliebs, with all their obvious money, would be into driving a family off the road, then stealing the children.

Back inside my Charger, I think about calling Lucas with the information.

"What information?" I ask myself. A very popular type of car with something that may or may not be a sticker that I may or may not have also seen on the kidnapper's car is not information.

Lucas might not laugh at my call, but Dustin certainly will.

I need to find out more. I need to get over the fence so I can see the car up close.

With sudden inspiration, I start the Charger, flinching at the loud rumble, I remind myself for the hundredth time that I need a new muffler. Once my shop in town gets up and running, maybe I'll have the cash to fix it. For now, I just shudder at how much noise the car makes.

I slowly pull the Charger off the road and park it parallel to the fence. The moment the car is close enough, I kill the engine. I wait a moment to be sure I haven't alerted any one inside. The house remains dark inside and none of the curtains move.

My coast is as clear as it will get.

I'm parked too close to the fence to open the driver's door. Climbing awkwardly over the center console and into the passenger seat, I manage to get out of the car. Only now do I think about the tracks I left in the snow around the perimeter fence and now the tire tracks in the strip of grass between the road and the fence. There's no way to hide that I've been here.

Deciding that is a problem for the Gottlieb's in the morning when they see them, I climb onto the hood of my car, then onto the roof. Trying not to think of any scratches or dents I may be causing to my precious

Charger, I grip the fence bars. From here, I can reach the top bar of the fence with my boot. I step on the bar, and shift my weight.

The fall to the snowy ground inside doesn't take long, but my mind still had time to remember something on the way down. "How will I get back over?"

Deciding I'll deal with that once I get the information I need, I brush the snow off my jeans and hurry to the parking area and the car in question.

Although it is a light colored, four door sedan, once I'm close to it, I know it's not the same car. I've been over and over the car in my memory and besides the sticker in the back side window, *or snow?*, the car in question also had a slightly different rim on the front tire as opposed to the back. From my vantage point of running through the field, I could only see one side of the car, but I'm almost certain the two rims I could see were not identical.

The car before me is immaculate and very new. The chrome shines in the holiday lights and the white paint is spotless. The wheel wells are not full of dirty, slushy, snow as they would have been if driving around the countryside looking for the children.

The sticker in the back passenger window has the same odd shape as the thing I saw on the kidnapper's car. On closer inspection, I realize the shape is an anchor. The sticker is from Barr Harbor Beach Club, another pretentious name.

I've never been to the "beach club," but I know what it is and I'm not surprised the Gottlieb's have property there. Barr Harbor is not a club at all, it's a high end, gated community on Harper Lake north of here about half an hour. Barr Harbor boasts fancy houses, boat slips and the whole resort life concept, at least as much as Indiana can offer such a thing.

Disappointed this car isn't the one that took the kids, I at least feel that the Barr Harbor Beach Club sticker has to be a lead. Why else would my tattoo bring me here?

My tattoo isn't tingling at all now, so maybe I'm grasping at straws with my tired mind. In a last ditch effort for some kind of sign, I take off my left glove and place my hand on the hood of the car.

Nothing useful. I grasp the driver's handle, hoping for a closer connection.

I do get a vague sense.

An older man, tired, disappointed. Kids couldn't be bothered to come again this year.

I let go of the handle, filled with sadness for Mr. Gottlieb. I'd imagined the Gottliebs must be a large family, or at least more than one old man. This huge estate, money coming out of his ears, and even his car handle tells me he's lonely and bitter.

The thought fills me with despair. There's no way this tired old man has Oliver, Cora and Ian.

I try one more thing with the car and place my bare hand flat on the Barr Harbor sticker. I push my skin into the cold plastic, open my mind and beg God for any sign or direction.

A tingle surges up my arm, but fades before it reaches my shoulder. A vision of the pink bear with the huge eyes I found in the back seat of the car flits through my mind.

That's it. A tingle and a toy bear. Basically nothing.

Discouraged and cold, my tired mind gives up on the car and thinks of my bed at Grandma's farm. There's nothing else I can do tonight, sleep is the only option.

But first I have to get back over the fence.

I survey my options of escape. I already know the fence encompasses the entire estate, tall and un-climbable on all four sides. I wonder if I can somehow push my feet through the bars and against the Charger and reverse rappel my way back over. I'm sure someone could do that, but my track record with coordination isn't good. It's my only option, so I at least give it a try.

I grip a bar in each hand and push my boots against the car door on the other side. The car isn't as close to the fence as I need it to be for this to work. I manage to get a few steps up the side, but then fall back to the snow.

I stomp the snow in frustration. The earlier storm dropped several inches, maybe I could roll the snow into balls the way you do to make a snowman, pile the balls up and use them to climb over.

It's a wild idea, but the only one I can think of. I drop to my knees and start rolling, realizing that I haven't made a snowman for years. One winter a few years ago, I got inspired on a Saturday home alone and made one in my front yard. I was proud of my little friend, even if I was way too old to be building snowmen by myself. With an unusual need for whimsy, I even put a pair of my gloves on his branch hands.

The cute little guy survived for only two days. When I got home from work on Monday, he was shattered. Some horrible person either kicked him to death or hit him with a bat. I suspected it was kids out to torture the *freak*. His branch arms were snapped into pieces and my gloves were gone. The kids probably took them as souvenirs from the horrible trick.

I took the loss of that snow friend much harder than an adult woman should. Teasing me, whispering behind my back, even vandalizing my house, those things I'd become accustomed to.

Killing my only friend, even if he was just made of snow, really hurt.

I roll the growing ball through the snow, and block out the memory of the last time I did this. The freshly fallen snow, mixed with the icy crystals that came towards the end of the storm, are not the best for making a snow ball that grows when you roll it.

Just when I start to despair that the idea isn't going to work and I need to find another plan, the decision to stop playing in the snow is made for me.

I see the black shape speeding through the yard towards me, before I hear it's growl. Normally, I love dogs and they love me. This Doberman is in no mood for getting to know me as a person. He seems intent on finding out what I taste like.

I scramble to my feet and run from the dog, not sure where I can go for safety. Some trees grow near the fence in the corner of the yard. They are the only protection I see, so I sprint for them.

I have a big head start on the dog, but he's way faster than I am. Running in a blind panic, I reach the first tree and jump as high as I can onto the trunk. My boots skitter against the bark, desperate for purchase to help me climb. The landscaper has been doing a good job of trimming the lowest branches, leaving knobby remains for me to push my toes against. I grasp the lowest branches and pull with all my strength.

Somehow, I get my butt onto a branch, pulling my feet up high away from the snapping dog. Panting from the exertion, I watch the dog jump against the tree, desperate to get to me.

"Good boy," I coo, hoping to calm him down. "You treed me good."

The dog isn't impressed with my flattery. He finally sits at the base of the tree and stares at me. Every few moments he growls.

"A psychic in a pear tree," I say out loud, laughing hysterically. I feel a panic attack niggling. My chest grows tight and my ears start to ring. The dog cocks his head as if confused by the strange noises I'm making.

"You're just a dog, you know," I tell him, trying to talk myself out of the panic. "I mean, you're not the friendliest dog I've ever met, but I bet you're a sweetie when you want to be."

The dog stops growling and lies down at the base of the tree, his head positioned so he can keep an eye on me.

"It's cold out here," I continue, shifting uncomfortably on the branch that's digging into my rear. "Wouldn't you rather be safe and warm in your dog house or wherever you sleep?"

He flickers his ears but has no intention of moving.

The branch is cutting off the circulation to my legs and an uncomfortable pressure is growing in my bladder. Maybe he's calmed down enough that he'll let me out of the tree. I make a move to climb down, testing him. He's instantly back on his feet, growling and snarling for me to stay put.

I resume my place on the branch and do the only thing I can think of.

I call Grandma Dot for help.

Chapter 10

GRANDMA DOT

When Emily shakes me awake, I'm sure her presence in my bedroom is a wonderful dream, not a wonderful reality. After years of my daughter being locked in prison for a murder that never happened, I'd given up hope of her ever returning home. The lovely blond woman shaking my shoulder must be an apparition summoned by my longing heart.

"Mom, wake up," Emily says. She's real, and solid, and shoving me hard in the shoulder.

My small black dog, Jet, stirs beside me, woken by the harsh shaking.

"What's wrong?" I ask groggily. "Are you sick?"

She holds the handset from the shop phone out to me. "Gabby needs you."

I push up into a seated position and click on the lamp. I squint against the sudden brightness, but not before I see a sly smile on Emily's lips.

"Gabriella, are you okay?" I rub my hand against my mess of curls.

"I'm fine. Well, not fine exactly, but I'm not hurt or anything."

My shoulders sink in relief. Middle of the night calls from Gabriella aren't exactly scarce events, but they scare me just the same.

I notice Emily is trying hard to control her smile. "Your mom is about to break out laughing, so maybe you better tell me what's up."

"I'm sort of stuck up in a tree."

It takes a moment for the words to sink in. Emily covers her mouth with her hand and swallows a giggle.

"Then climb down," I say irritated. "You're not a cat."

"Well," she draws the word out long, "I'm sort of like a cat at the moment. A dog chased me up here and he won't let me down."

Emily can hear every word and loses her battle against laughter. The small sounds of her happiness fills my heart and I can't help laughing too.

Gabby doesn't find it as funny. "This isn't really a laughing matter, Grandma. I'm in trouble here."

"I know, I'm sorry." I force my face into a sober expression. "What do you want me to do?"

"I'm just around the corner at the Gottlieb Estate. Can you bring me a ladder?"

"Why in the world are you in a tree at Ezra Gottlieb's? Don't tell me now, you can explain after we get you out."

"So you'll come?"

The question hurts my feelings a little. "Have I ever not come to rescue you?"

"No. Why do you think I called? Of course, you didn't answer your cell the first two times so I had to call the shop. Luckily Mom was up to answer."

I look on the nightstand for my cell, but it's not in its usual place. "Not sure where my phone is. Just hold tight and we'll be right there."

"Thanks, Grandma. Oh, can you bring some hot dogs or something?"

"Are you that hungry?"

"Not for me, for the dog. I have an idea."

Gabriella hangs up before I can ask anything else. I look to Emily, who's still smiling.

"She's changed," Emily says, pleased. "I mean, she was always a bit sassy as a child, but dogs chasing her into a tree in the middle of the night, on Christmas Eve no less? My girl's got guts."

"You have no idea how much she's changed." I climb out of bed and start changing clothes. "Want to come with me?"

"I wouldn't miss it." She skips out of the room. Her youthful movements trigger memories of her as a child. She had been an easy child, always happy and eager for fun. She looks more like that child than the middle-aged woman tonight. After losing fifteen years of her life in maximum security, everything delights her now.

I say a quick prayer, "God, thank You beyond measure for bringing my daughter back to me. Thank You for not letting her spirit break in that place. We are blessed beyond measure." Almost as an afterthought, I quickly say. "And help Gabriella out of whatever mess she's in tonight. I know You lead her where You need her to be, but please protect her. Amen."

"You coming, Mom?" Emily calls up the stairs. She's so excited to be on an adventure, especially one involving Gabriella, it's contagious.

Jet bounces at my feet, caught up in the mood too. "You can't come. If there's a big dog that has Gabby scared, you'd be a one bite snack to him."

"I've got the hot dogs," Emily calls impatiently.

"I think there's some meatballs in a Tupperware, too." I enter the kitchen and stop in my tracks when I see Emily. "What are you wearing?"

Her grin nearly breaks her face, highlighted by dark streaks from some kind of make-up. She's dressed head to toe in black, even has her light blonde hair tucked into a black knit cap. "You look like a ninja, or a bank robber."

"Exactly. Thought I'd dress the part."

I kiss her on her make-up streaked cheek. "Don't worry, getting Gabriella out of scrapes becomes part of the routine after a while."

"But tonight we're breaking her out from behind a fence. You have no idea how many times I dreamed of escaping over the fence, how many schemes and plans I created in my mind. Tonight we're breaking my daughter out. I can't believe it. I'll start the truck and get the ladder." She turns on her heel, the Tupperware of meatballs and the package of hot dogs under her arm.

By the time I get my boots on and button my coat, (all regular colored, I'm not dressing as a ninja), and walk onto the back porch, Emily is securing the ladder in the running flat bed truck.

She looks beautiful in the lights from the

back porch. She's still too thin, but has gained some weight. Her color under the make-up streaks is still pale, but it's lost the gray tones it had. The look of sadness and pain she carries everyday still lurks in her eyes.

My daughter is still the most beautiful thing in the world.

"Can I drive?" She sounds like she did when she had her learner's permit, begging to drive whenever we went anywhere. She'd learned to drive in this same flatbed, but hasn't been behind the wheel of any vehicle in years.

"Think you can still handle the clutch? It's grown touchier over the years."

"That wasn't a *no*." She runs around the hood of the running truck and climbs in, practically bouncing in the driver's seat.

It's been years since I've been a passenger in my own truck, and the bench seat feels odd under me, stiffer and less worn.

Emily puts the truck into reverse and I pretend not to notice the gears grinding. "Crap on a cracker," she exclaims.

I laugh out loud and worry about my

future. "You sound like Gabriella. Between the two of you, I'm not sure I can keep up."

The gears grind again as she forces the shifter into first and pulls forward. The truck stalls and she looks at me guiltily. "I can't even make the truck go forward, I think you can keep up."

I cover her hand on the stick shift, the way I did when she was first learning to drive. With my instruction, she gets us on the road and we roar and grind our way to the Gottlieb Estate. Luckily it's not too far, or my old truck may not have survived the trip.

Gabriella's Charger is parked in the grass, right next to the fence, not on the side of the road where it should be. For some reason Emily takes the truck out of gear and slides through the grass towards the Charger.

"Brake, brake," I shout. She randomly pushes on the pedals, so I grab the shifter and I force it into first. My beloved flatbed lurches, then stops a few inches from the fence. The Charger is so close, I can't see it over the hood of my truck.

"Sorry, Mom." Emily says. "I thought I should park where she did. I didn't expect to slide in the snow."

Her exuberant mood has deflated and I want it to return. "Well, parking on the road would have been fine, but this works too." I pat her hand that still grips the shifter. "We'll practice tomorrow, don't worry about it." I turn my attention to the windshield. "Kill the headlights. The house is still dark, so hopefully Ezra is sound asleep, but let's not wake him."

The beams of the headlights shine on a group of trees several yards away. Just before they go out, I glimpse a movement, a spot of red waving from up in a tree.

Without the headlights, the trees are hidden in shadow. "I think I saw her. Let's go." The creak from the door sounds amazingly loud in the hushed quiet of the snow covered night.

Emily's door is too close to the fence to open, so she slides across the bench seat and gets out on my side. "I've got the hot dogs and meatballs," she whispers loudly. I'm glad to hear her excitement is back.

Snow crunches under our boots as we follow what must be Gabriella's foot prints down the fence. As we approach the trees, the dog holding her there begins to growl. We take a few more slow steps, and the dog snarls at the fence. In the semi-darkness, the Doberman looks terrifying. I drive past this estate at least once a week and have seen this same dog playing in the yard. He's not a mean dog, he's just got a job to do and he's doing it well.

"Good boy," I say to him. "What a good job you're doing." He stops snarling, but holds his body stiff, watching us intently.

The wave of red moves in the tree again. "See why I couldn't get down," Gabriella says. "He wants to eat me."

"He doesn't want to eat you," Emily says, "He just wants you to leave."

"Then help me leave," she pleads. "My butt is going numb and I need to pee."

"We'll help you, but only if you tell us why in the world you'd break into this poor old man's property in the middle of the night." I'm all for helping her out, but this is a bit ridiculous, even for her. "You should be sound asleep with Lucas, or at least at home in your own bed."

Her voice is flat as she says, "I thought maybe the car back there was the one that kidnapped some kids." The tree rustles the few leaves that remain on the branch. "I'll explain all about it, but please hurry. I'm about to wet my pants up here."

Chapter 11

GABBY

When Mom answered the phone I'd been pleased and surprised. I knew Grandma would come help me, but I wasn't sure how Mom would react. Judging by her ninja outfit and the obvious enjoyment on her face, she reacted just fine. Having another person in my life who is willing to help me out, no questions asked, is amazing. They'll understand my reasons once I tell them about the car wreck and the missing kids.

They didn't know that yet, and still they came.

My bladder is giving me fits and my legs are nearly numb from sitting on this branch, so I start giving orders. "Good to see you already put the flatbed near the fence. That should help."

Mom smacks Grandma on the arm in a playful way. "See, I was right."

"Do you think you two can place the ladder on this side of the fence if you are standing on the flatbed?"

"I think I've been handling ladders and my flatbed since long before you were born," Grandma says a bit testily.

"Great," I say breezily. "Once you get the ladder in place, then take the hot dogs…."

"Ooh, and tempt the dog away from you. I get it." Mom is excited about the plan. "I'll do that part."

I try to squeeze my legs together against the building pressure in my bladder. "Please hurry," I plead.

They crunch away to set up the ladder. It bangs against the metal fence, but I can see from here it's standing upright. The dog is pacing anxiously between me and the ladder, wanting to guard us both.

"Come here, doggy," Mom says. I can see her clearly at the fence, her all black outfit standing out against the bright white snow everywhere. Her hand is through the fence and she's dangling a hot dog.

The dog looks at the treat then at me. "Go get it, boy. You know you want it," I urge.

Mom tosses the hot dog towards the dog. He gobbles it in one bite. She sticks another through the gate and dangles it enticingly.

He takes a step or two towards the offered meat, but checks on me over his shoulder.

Mom tosses the hot dog and it lands about ten feet in front of him.

He sniffs the snow, and slowly, stiffly moves towards the treat. Once he finds it, he gobbles it up and looks to Mom for more. She's ready and throws another instantly and closer to her, farther from the tree.

The dog doesn't look over his shoulder at me this time, just goes for the treat. Mom keeps tossing hot dogs and leading the dog further away, all the while telling him what a good boy he is and how he doesn't need to worry about the girl in the tree.

The girl in the tree begins climbing to the

ground. I move as silently as possible, trying not to draw the dog's attention. I make it to the ground, but hesitate moving away from the safety of the tree. Mom runs out of hot dogs and switches to meatballs. She and the dog are at the far end of the yard now and the ladder is closer to me than to him.

"You ready to run, Gabby?" Mom asks, using the same sing-song voice she's been charming the dog with. "I'm going to give him a bunch of meatballs, and then you are going to run like hell, aren't you girl?" she coos.

Meatballs start pelting the snow and I sprint towards the ladder. I make it half way there before the dog even notices I've moved. Once he sees me, he forgets all about the treats.

The dog and I both sprint to the ladder. I'm closer, but he's much faster. Grandma yells for me to run, Mom tries to recapture the dog's attention.

I scramble up the ladder, making it half way up before the dog reaches me. His body slams into the ladder and it slides in the snow. Grandma squeals as the ladder teeters dangerously.

I don't think, I just climb. I get high enough to place a boot on the top bar of the fence, the same way I got over. I shove with all my strength on that leg and vault over.

The hard wood of the flatbed slams into me, nothing like the soft landing in the snow I had on the way in. My shoulder took most of the impact and aches deep in the joint. Most of the air was knocked out of my lung on impact. I roll on my back and stare at the moonlight filtering through the clouds overhead as I gasp for breath.

Grandma is at my side. "Couple deep breaths, and you'll be fine." I can barely hear her over the barking of the dog.

I rub my sore shoulder and gasp the cold air.

"Holy crap that was cool!" Mom says suddenly next to the flat bed. "You jumped right over it. What a night." I turn my head to see her smile. She tosses another meatball at the dog. "Be quiet, she's already out." He snaps the meatball up and thankfully stops barking. He just paces the fence, making a mix of a whine and a growl.

Once I catch my breath, I sit up and slide off the truck bed. "Excuse me."

I can't hold it any longer. I hurry around to where the truck and the Charger are close together for some privacy, then unbutton my jeans and squat.

"Good Lord, Gabriella. We're less than a mile from home. Couldn't you hold it?"

Before I can answer, a "whoop-whoop" from a cop car cuts through the night. No lights, no sirens, we hadn't noticed its approach and it pulls to a stop behind the truck. The headlights shine under the truck and I feel exposed. As quickly as I can, I finish my business and pull my pants back up.

Mom has gone still, a look of terror on her face. "Your son is the head detective in this town," I whisper in her ear. "Not to mention Lucas. You have nothing to worry about."

Her stiffness loosens a fraction, but she hangs her head and assumes a posture of obedience. I don't like the look on her.

The cruiser door opens and I recognize the officer as the one that helped me the night Dustin was shot. I'm pretty sure he was at the wreck scene earlier tonight, too, but I'm not sure.

"Hey, good to see you again," I say breezily as if we are at a party or something. "Officer Patterson, right?"

"Gabby McAllister, I was afraid that was you." He sounds amused, not annoyed. "Dot, I'd recognize this trunk from anywhere." Grandma's still standing on the flatbed, shielding her eyes from the glare of the headlights. Mom is between the truck and the fence not making a move, and Patterson hasn't noticed her yet. The dog just stands inside the fence, watching.

"Best truck in the county," Grandma says just as friendly as I was. Patterson reaches inside the cruiser and turns off the headlights. White dots float in my eyes every time I blink.

The diffused moonlight and the massive light display offer enough illumination for him to see us. Grandma reaches for his hand to help her down from the bed of the truck. She even groans as she climbs down, making a fuss for attention. She even adds, "Thank you, young man," for good measure.

Patterson helps Grandma to the ground, then his eyes drift over my mom and her face paint and dark clothes. He opens his mouth to talk to her, but I interrupt.

"What brings you way out here this late at night, Officer Patterson?" I sound innocent, but inside I'm shaking.

He cocks his head towards the big house and says, "You wanna guess?"

"I was investigating," I say quickly.

"You were trespassing," he corrects. "You're lucky Mr. Gottlieb only let his dog outside on you and isn't the type to own a gun." He looks towards the house again and waves. In a shadowed corner of the porch, where the light display can't reach, a gray haired man waves back. A whistle echoes across the snowy yard and the dog runs to his master.

I'm shocked that we've been being

watched this entire time. "How long has he been out there watching us?" I ask with indignation.

"It's his property, he can watch as long as he wants," Patterson replies. He looks at Grandma then back at me, shuffles his feet in the snow. "I want to believe you have a good reason for this. Especially in light of what happened earlier. If you don't want Mr. Gottlieb to press charges, you better start talking."

"What happened earlier?" Grandma asks, her tone sharp. "Gabriella, what is all this about?"

I look to Patterson for help. Between the two of us, we explain about the car wreck, how I saw the kids taken away in a four door sedan. How I thought maybe the car in the driveway was the one that had the kids.

"I had to know for sure." I finish my story. "If he wants to press trespassing charges, I understand, but I had no choice."

Mom hasn't said a word the entire time, but she speaks up now. "You will not be going to jail, not for any reason. You will not be arresting her." A strange energy, a fierce strength flashes through her. I get a sense that we're seeing a glimpse of the Emily she has been forced to be for the last fifteen years.

Patterson stares at her for a moment, shocked by her sudden outburst. I have no doubt he knows who she is. The entire town of River Bend has been talking about my mom's release from prison. Most people are pleased that justice was finally served. A few nasty people think she's a criminal just for spending time in prison, even if she was innocent going in.

I wonder which camp Patterson is in.

"Don't worry, ma'am." His voice is respectful and reassuring. I breathe a sigh of relief. It's bad enough half the police force think I'm a kook, I don't want them judging my mom, too. At least Patterson seems to be on our side. He continues, "I'm sure once I explain to Mr. Gottlieb about the complete situation and why Gabby climbed over, he'll be more than understanding. I'm sure he wants the children found, too."

"So Lucas and Dustin haven't found anything new?" I ask. I've been trying to leave them to their work, but I'm dying to know what's going on."

"Patrol's been quiet tonight, so I've been following their progress on the radio. They talked to Lauren Whitlow's mother. Jared Whitlow was found at his apartment and the kids weren't with him. McAllister and Hartley are interviewing him now. That's really all I know."

"So nothing. Crap."

Patterson rubs the back of his neck and looks towards the ground. "Have you got any ideas? I mean, I know what you do, I've seen it up close. Do you know anything we don't?"

I almost laugh at his stammering, but I'm too pleased at being asked. "I remember seeing what was either a sticker or a patch of snow on the car. That car there looked similar and has the same sticker. Once I touched the car, I knew the kids weren't here. But when I touched the sticker, I got a flash of one of the little girl's toys I saw in the wrecked car."

All three of them stare at me for a moment. Mom's mouth is hanging open and she shuts it with a quiet snap. "You got that from touching a sticker?"

I shrug, uncomfortable by her obvious admiration. "It's not really anything. I do think the stickers are related somehow, though."

"What is it?" Patterson asks.

"It's a membership sticker for the Barr Harbor Beach Club. You know, that super ritzy lake community up by Vinton."

Grandma gasps suddenly. "Barr Harbor. I know someone who has a place up there. You won't believe it." She fairly glows with the information.

The three of us say in unison, "Who?"

Grandma is so pleased with herself, she draws out the moment. "Paula Whitlow. She comes in for a quick trim once in a while. Although she normally goes to one of those overly expensive salons in Fort Wayne. She's constantly bragging about something or other. She talks about her lake house up at Barr

174

Harbor Beach Club."

"Paula Whitlow," Patterson says. "Any relation to Jared?"

Grandma beams with pride again. "She's his mom."

My blood churns with excitement. "The kids would definitely have gotten into a car with their grandma. Does she drive a light colored sedan?"

Grandma's face drops and she shakes her head. "I've only seen her in a massive SUV."

"Not a sedan with one rim that doesn't match the others?" I ask desperately.

Grandma shakes her head. "Just the big black thing."

I turn my eyes to Patterson. "It can't be a coincidence," I plead. "I felt something from that sticker," I point to the car in the driveway. "It's related to the kids somehow."

"I agree, but what do you want me to do about it? I'm just patrol."

Excited now that I have a direction to move in, I say, "Tell Lucas and Dustin about the link as soon as you can. Have them ask the kid's dad about it and get me an address. If they are in an interview right now, I can't call them, but you should be able to get the message through. As Lucas to text me Paula's address once he gets it."

"I'll try," Patterson says. "What are you going to do?"

"You're coming home, right?" Grandma Dot asks, but she already knows the answer.

"I'm going to Barr Harbor. Tell Lucas and Dustin to come when they're done."

Mom still holds the container with a few meatballs left in it, and I take it from her. She lets me have it eagerly, even gives me the lid. "Are you hungry?"

I share a smile with her. Growing up, she'd ask me that all the time. It's pretty standard mom-words, but I know it was her way of opening a conversation and showing me she cared at the same time. "Won't be after I eat these. You don't happen to have any sodas in the truck do you?" I ask Grandma.

"Gabriella, you're not driving up to Barr Harbor now. It's an hour away and the middle of the night."

I slip a glove off and pluck a cold meatball out of the juice at the bottom. "So?" I say through a mouthful of food. "I'm not going to go home and pretend to sleep. Not when I might be able to find the kids." I pop another meatball in my mouth, then snap the lid back on. "Sodas? Or even coffee. I need some caffeine." I lick the cold sauce off my fingers.

Grandma hangs her head. "There's still some in the thermos from this morning." She pulls the door of the truck open and it squeaks loudly. Finding the thermos on the floorboard, she hands it to me. I give it a shake, it feels about half full.

I twist off the cap and down a few drinks of the ice cold coffee. It tastes terrible, but it will help keep me awake.

Patterson has watched all this in silence, but he clears his throat now. "Um, we have the little matter of the trespass call," he says. "Mr. Gottlieb is still sitting on his porch waiting for me to arrest you."

Mom stiffens and steps between me and

Patterson. I take another drink of the awful coffee, then say, "I'm sure you will figure out something to tell him. If you still want to arrest me tomorrow, come find me. Right now, I've got work to do."

I give a quick hug to Mom and to Grandma then head for my Charger.

"Aren't you going to stop her from going?" Mom asks Grandma and Officer Patterson at the same time.

"Go ahead and try," Grandma says. "I've learned it's best to let her do her thing. She usually wins in the end."

The rumble of my engine drowns out whatever else they say about me. My tires kick up snow as I pull away from the fence. I give a little wave and a shrug as if to say *sorry*, then speed off towards the interstate.

Grandma's right, Barr Harbor Beach Club is nearly an hour drive away. I plug my phone in to radio and key up my favorite playlist. It's the one I usually jog to, not that I've had time or inclination to jog since the weather has turned cold. "Thriller" by Michael Jackson begins. As soon as I hear the creaking door and echoing footsteps, I get excited.

With the music turned as loud as it will go, I sing along, my hips dancing in the seat. With good music playing and Grandma's cold coffee giving me a caffeine rush, the miles flash by. I have no idea what I'll do once I get to Barr Harbor Beach Club. Hopefully Lucas will have texted me the address I need. If not, I'll figure something out.

The song ends and I hit repeat. "Cause this is Thriller!"

Not exactly Christmas music, but even better.

Chapter 12

GABBY

The tunes and the coffee keep me going, but I'm butt-dragging tired when I finally take the exit off I-69 that leads to Barr Harbor Beach Club. The club is nestled along the shore of Harper Lake just outside the quaint town of Vinton, IN. When we were kids, our parents brought Dustin and me to Vinton to swim at the beach and have lunch at the boardwalk. For rural Indiana, it was pretty cool. Near the highway, Vinton is like any other town, closer to the frozen lake, the old-style downtown has retained its charm.

The town square with the obligatory center courthouse is smaller than the square in River Bend where my shop is located, but it oozes nostalgia. Vinton is a tourist town trying desperately to resemble a Hallmark Channel movie. A lighted nativity fills one side of the center courtyard and a massive tree sits on the other. I've heard rumors of the events they have here at the holidays, tree lighting, live nativity, even an ice carving contest. The results of the contest are on display around the courtyard, the ice twinkling in the lights hung in the trees.

Each shop around the center has also joined in the fun, trying to pull in a few extra tourist dollars before the harsh grip of Indiana winter. Colorful window displays, complete with lights fill most of the windows.

The entire view is almost perfect.

The view from my shop, "Messages," looks a lot different. I didn't even put lights up at the shop, although some other stores did. Our courthouse did change the floodlights to red and green bulbs, but that's the only change. The idea of what could be at home makes me sad.

A huge yawn interrupts my thoughts. Vinton may be beautiful, and maybe next year Lucas and I can come for some of the activities, but right now I have to stay alert and focused.

And search for the kids.

On the edge of town, I find the tasteful gates and massive wooden sign of Barr Harbor Beach Club. On the drive, I'd worried the gates would be closed and locked. Half-way here, I'd given the worry to God. If He needed me to just drive through the open gate, I would. If He needed me to climb a fence, well I've already done that once tonight. An encore performance wouldn't be a big deal.

Relieved, I drive through the open gate.

The club consists of one road that winds along the lake shore. Huge homes on the lake side have their own private docks, private beaches. Most of the houses on that side are dark, except for the occasional night light. I don't need to have my gift to sense the houses are empty this time of year. Anyone with the kind of money it takes to own a lake house like that is probably spending the holidays somewhere much more exotic, or at least warm.

The off-lake side is still impressive by most standards, but the houses pale compared to the lake-side estates and the lots are much smaller. The occasional house has a lived in year round vibe. With any luck one of them belongs to Paula Whitlow.

With even better luck, I'll find the kids safe and sound with their Grandma and all of this is some horrible misunderstanding.

No amount of luck will bring their mother or her boyfriend back to life.

That thought makes my chest hurt.

No matter what happens tonight, Christmas will never be the same for those kids.

Life will never be the same.

I lost my mom at 14, but at least I knew she was alive, just locked away from me.

I lost my dad the same night. Beyond the grief, that turned out to be horrible layer after layer.

"Just be safe, and we'll deal with the rest later," I whisper to the kids.

I drive the length of the neighborhood and I down the rest of the acid, cold, coffee. At the far end, the lane ends at a community area. The beach club.

The beach is covered in snow, the lake beyond frozen with a thin layer of ice. A small marina stretches into the ice on the far side of the beach. I imagine each slot can be rented by the off-lake residents. There's a small building between the beach and the marina. Some sort of boat house or storage place. I squint at the building again, not understanding, then see the ice cream cone shaped sign. Of course, a snack-shack. Even a private club has to sell snacks.

I park at random in the lot of unplowed asphalt. The cloud cover had thickened on my drive up here and the moon is nearly indistinguishable in the darkness. The beams of my headlights slice through the dark and illuminate a set of swings on an elaborate play center. Wooden towers complete with bridges, climbing ropes, slides and swings sits empty and forlorn in the snow covered play area. I can see four swings in my headlights, but only one of them moves back and forth as if a ghost was having a go.

If it's a ghost, I'm not getting a sense from it. But ghosts are not my specialty.

The single moving swing holds my attention, the red seat floating back and forth, the color bright against the white of the snow. The other three swings are still, the red one picks up speed. Mesmerized, I watch it until a violent shake jumps through me.

Unnerved, I put the Charger in reverse and park on the other side of the lot, away from the swings. The entire beach club is covered in fresh snow, powdery and blowing, not the harsh icy snow we got farther south.

I turn off my roaring engine and the wind from the lake blows snow against my windshield, bright fat flakes, reflected in the light. I switch off the lights.

Quite fills the beach club area.

Quiet fills my car.

Quiet is my tattoo.

I check my phone again, hoping for an address from Lucas or even from Officer Patterson. Either Lucas hasn't gotten the message, or has chosen not to tell me the address of Paula Whitlow.

A misguided hope to keep me safe.

Lucas should know me better.

Frustrated, I tuck my silent phone into my back jeans pocket and climb into the cold. I'll find her house and if the kids are here, I'll find them.

He works his way.

I work mine.

I pull the red hood from Grandma's Christmas hoodie to cover my curls and tie it against the cold. I then pull my coat hood up and zip my coat as high as it will go. At least I'm wearing hiking boots, not my dress boots that I ran through the woods in. So far, my toes are warm. I pull on the mismatched gloves, wishing I had thick winter gloves to wear. My good pair is at home on the table near my front door. If I'd known I would be walking around in the freezing cold of pre-dawn, I might have grabbed them on my way out.

I can hear the swing still moving behind me, the chain rattling in the dark. I make a point not to look at it.

Instead, I turn my face to the overcast sky and talk to God. "Please show me what You need me to see. Please guide my feet where You need them to go."

Lucas once told me that shoes on the ground is the basis of all police work. Canvassing a neighborhood takes time, but is essential in an investigation.

I might not have a team of cops to help with my canvas, but I'm here and willing to do the work. With my mind open to the universe, searching, straining to hear, I start my trek up the lane.

The first few houses are dark and I know they are empty, so I keep walking. When I come to a house that seems it might have an occupant, I realize the major problem with my plan.

Police can bang on doors in the middle of the night if they need to. If I bang on this door and start asking questions, the police will be here, but not for the reason I need them.

I stand on the road, outside the house I

think someone is sleeping inside and check my phone once again for an address. If I at least knew which house was Paula's I'd have an almost legitimate reason to knock on her door.

My phone is still blank. Not even an early Merry Christmas text from my only friend, Haley.

I hover my blue and pink striped finger over the contact for calling Lucas. He's probably still interviewing the drunk dad of the missing kids. I don't want to interfere. I don't have Officer Patterson's number, and kick myself for not getting it while I was with him. He could look up the woman's address for me on their system.

I scroll through the phone and find Haley's number. We used to be work friends. After I got fired, she surprised me by wanting to be actual friends. She's also a wiz at finding information on the internet, sometimes even info the cops can't find.

Before I bother her, I do a quick Google of Paula Whitlow, hoping her lake house address will be listed and easy to find. No such luck.

Hoping Haley cares for me enough to not hate me for calling her hours before Christmas Morning, I push the call button.

She's groggy and concerned, with a strong undercurrent of excitement when she answers. "If you're calling me at this hour, there must be something interesting going on," she says by way of hello.

I fill her in on the details of the night and what I need. Her excitement grows with each sentence. A single woman working at a catalog call center doesn't get much excitement in her life. Trust me, I know. Still, I feel guilty for waking her.

"I know it's super late, but I didn't know what else to do. I can't just start knocking on doors. And I'm sure these houses have security systems so I can't peak in all the windows and hope to get lucky."

"You're not bothering me at all." In the background, I hear clicking of keys. I can almost see her face scrunched with interest, her blond hair a mess from sleep. "Using my dusty skills to hopefully find some kidnapped children is the best gift you could give me."

"I got you an actual gift." I smile into the phone. "Guess now, I can take it back for a refund. Save a little money."

"You're not getting off that easily." More typing on her keyboard. I wait quietly, letting her work. A blast of lake air blows against my face, and I turn my back to it. "Do you want to call me back once you find something?"

"After all we've been through, you think a simple address was going to take all night?" Haley teases. The typing sounds have stopped.

"You found it already?"

"My gift to you. Looks like we both can return the actual gifts we bought." Haley rattles off the address and I check it against the number on the house I'm standing in front of. The numbers don't match. Paula's house is further up the street.

Truly thankful for her help, I make a request that a "normal" person would have no problem making. For me, it's a huge leap. "Or we could meet for a drink later and exchange gifts." Nerves flood my belly. Drinks with a friend in public? Am I nuts? Haley and I once had lunch together when we were co-workers. That was way out of my comfort range, but I'd enjoyed it. She came to my Grand Opening party and we talk on the phone sometimes. For me, that's the best friend I've had since Lucas's sister when we were kids. That friendship turned out tragically.

"Gabby McAllister, you want to go out and have some fun?" She teases. "Like a girl's night out?" I can hear her bright smile through the phone.

I feel my face grow warm against the freezing wind. "So," I say a little defensively. "It's not that crazy of an idea is it?"

Haley says sincerely, "It's not crazy at all. I'd love to. I was meeting a few other girls tomorrow, tonight, whatever day it is, anyway. Would you like to join us? They're nice. Good friends of mine."

Other women? What did I get myself into?

I swallow hard, and stammer, "Sure, I guess so." I start walking up the lane as Haley gives me the details, checking the house numbers. The walking does nothing to quell the anxiety of what most women would be looking forward to.

I'm not most women.

Most women aren't looking for a killer and a kidnapper in a ritzy lake home neighborhood right now.

Haley chats in her easy friendly manner as the numbers climb and I find myself standing at the end of Paula Whitlow's driveway. "I found the house," I interrupt her. "I've got to go."

"Gabby, wait." I put the phone back to my ear.

"Yeah?"

"What are you going to do? If she really did force that car off the road and take the kids, she could be dangerous. Can't you at least wait for Lucas or your brother, or even call the local cops?"

She has a point, but that's not my style, I take my order from only One, and He's tingling up my arm right now. I can't explain that to Haley.

I make a small sound that might pass for a laugh instead, "Tell you what, I'll try calling Lucas again."

Haley sounds relieved. "Be careful and I'll see you tonight right?"

My focus has shifted from our conversation to the section of Paula's front room I can see through her window. "Yeah, I'll be there."

I end the call with Haley and dial Lucas as I promised. I get his voice mail. "Crap on a cracker, Lucas," I snap into the phone walking up Paula's driveway. "I realize you're busy, but I sent you a message with Patterson over an hour ago and now I'm alone and freezing." Still on the phone, I get a better look into the front room. The tree is lit and presents fill the space underneath. On a wall nearby, three stockings are stuffed with goodies. Oliver, Ian and Cora written in golden glitter on the fuzzy cuffs.

The huge eyes of a small stuffed pink giraffe look at me from the stocking. The same type of huge eyes that looked at me from the

194

floorboard of the smashed car.

"I think I found the kids," I finish the call and hang up.

I promised Haley I'd call, but I didn't promise to wait.

My tattoo pulses in a pleasant staccato of sensation. I turn my face to the cold lake breeze and hold my eyes open until they tear up.

Then I pound on the front door of Paula Whitlow's lake house with panicked blows on the cold metal door. My knocks match the beat of my tattoo. I work my face up into a fearful expression and let the wind cause tears to flow down my cheeks.

"Is anyone home?" I shout in desperation. "Please, help me."

Chapter 13

LUCAS

By the time we confront Jared Whitlow in the interview room, he's shrunk to a shadow of himself. I know from my experience with mine and Amber's divorce a few years ago that the first Christmas is the hardest. This poor man struggled with that earlier this evening and he took the route many have taken before. Looking for release in a bottle.

The added losses of his soon to be ex-wife's death and the kidnapping of his children has nearly ruined him. The buttons of his shirt seem to be the only thing holding him upright.

As gently as possible, Dustin and I push him for information. Between blank stares and short, mumbled responses, we don't get very

197

far. He has no idea who would want to hurt Lauren and Eric or take his children.

Frustrated with the lack of progress, we finally call for a break. The poor man isn't going to be able to help us and further questioning feels like unnecessary torture.

I follow Dustin to the coffee corner and fill a cup. Long nights and endless hours are part of our jobs, but my eyes are beginning to burn with exhaustion. Dustin fills a cup for me and adds way too much sugar and cream. He likes it that way, I like mine a little more bitter. At least it's full of caffeine and still passably hot.

"Think we're going to get anything useful?" Dustin asks in the hallway.

I rub the stubble growth on my cheek and shake my head. "I think he's as shocked as we are."

We sip our coffee, both of us trying to find another angle to tackle. My stomach rumbles loudly, needing more than coffee to fill it.

Dustin hears the noise and doesn't miss the chance to tease me. "Too bad you dropped that cookie, maybe your stomach wouldn't be so loud."

The delicious looking cookie is no doubt a soggy pile in Teresa's driveway now. I need something to put in my belly and head down the hall to our office to search for some snacks in my desk, maybe some jerky.

Officer Patterson intercepts me on the way.

"How's the interview going?" he asks.

I make a sound and shrug. Patterson follows me to my office. I pull open a drawer and start rummaging around. The only thing I find that passes for food is an old stick of gum.

"Have you heard from Gabby?" he asks.

I stop rummaging, and turn my full attention to him. A shiver of warning climbs up my back. "Why would I have heard from Gabby? She's in bed asleep." I give myself a mental slap. She never said she was going to bed. I never saw her in bed. Did I really think my text about nothing she could do tonight would deter her?

Patterson links his thumbs in his belt, then pulls them out again, obviously uncomfortable.

I pull myself up to my full height although

I'm maybe half an inch taller than Patterson. "Spill it."

Dustin appears in the doorway to our office, his phone in his hand. He's about to say something, but sensing the thick tension in the room, he just watches.

Patterson stumbles through his story about Gabby and Grandma Dot and even Emily at the Gottlieb estate. As he speaks, he seems to grow shorter, deflated. My concern and anger fills me, swells me up with indignation.

Patterson ends his little story with letting Gabby drive away. "You didn't stop her?" I bellow.

To his credit, he squares his shoulders against me. "From the stories I've heard around here, you two can't stop her when she gets a mind to do something. You're her brother and you're her boyfriend, I barely know her."

I force my shoulders to relax. He's right. Trying to control Gabby is like trying to stop the snow. Better to just let it fall and shovel the mess up later.

"We have a bigger problem," Dustin says quietly. "The preliminary tox screen just came back on Lauren Whitlow. She was poisoned."

Our office is filled with a heavy sadness. A tiny surge of vindication fills my heart. It wasn't my fault Lauren Whitlow died. I didn't do anything wrong at the scene.

I suddenly feel guilty. The woman is dead. The children lost their mother, Teresa lost her daughter.

"What about Eric, was he poisoned too?"

Dustin shakes his head. "Just Lauren. The coroner checked her stomach and the only thing in there was the remains of flour and sugar."

My knees suddenly grow weak and I sink into my office chair. "Like a cookie? A poisoned cookie?"

Dustin nods gravely. "Thank God, Gabby texted you right then."

Patterson looks from me to Dustin, confused about the importance of the cookie.

I snap out of my shock. "Teresa said Paula Whitlow gave those cookies to Lauren. Gabby and Grandma Dot think Paula is at Barr Harbor Beach Club."

I shove away from my desk and storm down the hall to the interview room where Jared Whitlow lays with his head on his crossed arms on the table. I kick the table to wake him up.

"Your mom like to make cookies?" I bark.

He jumps awake and blinks several times. "Cookies?"

"Your mother, does she like making cookies, maybe sharing a tray of them with Lauren?"

"She bakes all the time. Why?"

"Tonight she gave Lauren a plate of poisoned cookies." I pause letting the fact sink into the mush of his mind. "She murdered her, not just forced her off the road."

"Mom, wouldn't do that," he protests without conviction.

Dustin asks, "Does your mother own property at Barr Harbor Beach Club in Vinton?"

Jared nods.

"Does she drive a four door light colored sedan?"

A spark of hope ignites in the broken man. "No, she drives an SUV. What's this all about? You think my mom did this?"

I lean so close to the man, I can smell the remains of alcohol and stress sweat on him. I lock eyes with his watery gray ones. "Do you think she has something to do with this?"

A slight tightening of his eyes gives him away. "I never thought she'd do *this*," he opens his arms wide, "but she was angry about the divorce, angry about me having to share the kids."

He crumbles as the truth crushes. "She killed Lauren and Eric. Lauren is precious, and Eric wasn't really that bad." He crosses his arms on the table and lowers his head again, sobbing.

A surge of pity for the man is replaced with worry for Gabby. She's driving north right now to confront a woman who'd use a cookie as a weapon. I bark orders at Patterson as I storm into my office again, "Go to Lauren

Whitlow's home and find her mother, Teresa. Warn her about the cookies and collect them all for evidence. Hopefully she hasn't eaten one, too."

I pull my coat from the back of my office chair. "There's one in the driveway, too. Make sure you get that picked up before the little dog gets to it."

Dustin has followed into the office and pulls on his own coat. "To Barr Harbor?" he asks.

"How long ago did she leave?" I ask Patterson. He looks at the clock on the wall, the red second hand ticking away the precious moments I need to get to Gabby. "It's been nearly an hour now," he says apologetically. "I got to you as soon as I could."

"Crap, she's probably already there now. At least she doesn't know which house is Paula's that should buy us some time."

I dig my phone out of my pocket, ready to call her and warn her. The screen is dead and no amount of stabbing at the buttons will resurrect it. I make a strangled sound of frustration. "Mine's dead," I tell Dustin. "You'll have to call her."

He tries, but gets no answer. Sends a text just in case.

Bustled in our coats we hurry down the hall of the precinct towards the parking garage and a cruiser that will take us north. Dustin is a few steps ahead of me, his empty sleeve, the one where his slinged arm should be, billows behind him. I watch as he fishes another pill out of his pocket and dry swallows it.

"I'll drive," I say, pushing the concern about his pill intake to the back of my mind.

He doesn't argue, which bothers me more than the pills. He shouldn't be on this case at all. He should be home recovering.

We should all be home.

But we need to find the kids and Gabby.

I say a prayer for a hedge of protection around us all.

With lights and sirens on, we speed out of River Bend and onto the Interstate.

I plug my phone in to the car charger and see the missed call and voicemail from Gabby.

Listening to her message only makes my fear grow.

I call back, but it goes directly to voicemail the same it did for Dustin.

"Don't do anything stupid before we get there," I say to Gabby's voicemail. "We're coming."

I follow up with a similar text.

Then I repeat my prayer of protection and fly down the interstate.

Chapter 14

GABBY

My frantic pounding eventually draws Paula Whitlow to the door. As the door opens a crack, I start my show.

"Oh my gosh, thank you for answering," I blubber. "Have you seen my Grandma's dog? I was supposed to be house sitting, and I let him out and he took off. I can't find him anywhere."

Paula rubs her tired, red bloodshot eyes in exasperation, not pleased with my intrusion before the sun is even up. "I haven't seen a dog."

She tries to close the door, but I've slid my boot into the gap. "I know he's close by, can you please help me find him. Grandma just adores the little guy and I should have taken better care of him. I got home late from a party and he needed to go out so bad, I just opened the door and he disappeared." I babble on and on, barely stopping to take a breath. "Frodo," I yell loudly into the night for the imaginary dog, "Frodo are you out here?"

My raised voice is irritating her now. "I already told you, there is no dog here." Distracted by my hysterics, Paula hasn't noticed my boot pushing the gap in the door wider. I look towards the tree and the stockings. The wide eyed pink giraffe smiles at me, cheering me on.

"I'm sorry to bother but I'm so desperate. Grandma will be home in the morning and if Frodo isn't here, she'll be heart-broken with it being Christmas and everything. She loves that dog like a child." I motion my head to the presents and stockings, "Maybe your kids have seen him?"

Paula is losing her patience and I'm not actually getting anywhere. It is possible that the kids are not in this house. She is the missing children's grandma, but she might not be involved. The gifts could be waiting for tomorrow innocently.

I take off my left glove and wipe the fake tears off my face with it. I cover my face with the glove and begin to sob. Paula softens a bit at my obvious distress and pats my shoulder.

Taking advantage, I grasp her bare hand with my bare left hand.

The swirl of darkness and evil intentions nearly knocks the air from my lungs.

Hatred claws at my chest, jealousy, longing, a need to control. A shout of triumph as the red car careens off the road, down the ditch and into the trees. What do you mean she has the kids?! Frantic searching. There they are. Mine, mine, mine, mine.....

Paula pries my hand off of hers one finger at a time. "Listen, lady, I don't know who you are or where your damn dog is, but you need to get off my property right now."

I'm so shaken by the vision I stumble backwards off her porch. "I'm sorry I bothered you," I say quietly, the imaginary Frodo forgotten and the need for me to escape strong.

"Which house did you say you are staying at?" she calls after me. "I know everyone who lives here during the winter and I've never seen you."

I return my hand to the safety of my glove and hurry down her driveway. My Charger is parked at the end of the lane, I turn in the opposite direction, not wanting to give her any clues. A few feet before I reach the road, I begin to run. I feel dirty and violated from the darkness I felt in the woman.

My feet pound the icy asphalt and my lungs burn from the cold air against the heat inside my chest. Growing warm from the jog, I let down the hood of my coat, and untie the hoodie from under my chin. My brown curls blow free in the wind coming from the lake. I lift my feet and slam them onto the asphalt, driving myself hard. During good weather, I run nearly every day, but I'm a bit out of shape now. It doesn't take long until I'm gasping for air and my legs are aching. I slow my desperate run to a sustainable jog.

By the time I reach the entrance gates of the neighborhood, I am true and surely tired. I lean against the wrought iron, gasping for air in the pre-dawn silence. Behind me, down the lane, I hear an engine, the only other car I've heard or seen since I drove through this gate earlier. I expect the car to be leaving, to pass me at the gate, the only entrance or exit from the Barr Harbor.

The motor sound grows dimmer, driving in the opposite direction.

I chase the sound, running as hard as I can. Through the dark, I see red taillights ahead. Low to the ground and close together, a car. No matter how hard I pump my legs, I can't catch up. The car disappears around the curves in the lane, headed towards the park and beach end of the neighborhood.

Unable to keep up the sprint, I slow again to what can only technically be called a jog it's so slow. As I pass Paula's house, I'm surprised to see that the only marks in the snowy driveway are my footprints from earlier. No car tracks.

The house next door is dark. The sidewalk hasn't been shoveled. All the curtains are pulled shut, and only a small light is on towards the back of the house. I sense no one is living there at the moment.

The snow in the driveway hasn't been plowed all season, judging by the evenness of the snow and the lack of piles at the edges.

The sets of tire tracks leading to and from the closed garage door don't make sense for a house that's not currently being lived in.

I slow my jog and look at the tracks. If I touched them, I'm sure I'd get a glimpse of the same car I saw hours ago picking up the kids.

Now that I'm not running, I notice the buzz in my pocket. Messages from both Lucas and Dustin fill my screen. I don't listen to the voicemails, the texts say enough.

The same thing they always tell me.

Sit still and wait for the men to handle things.

Irritated, I don't respond, leave the ringer off and shove the phone back in my pocket.

Paula's driven to the frozen beach with the kids. Judging by the horrible things I sensed inside her, there's no telling what her plans are.

Mine, mine, mine....

The memory of her thought makes bile rise to the back of my throat. The woman is disturbed, and she has three defenseless children with her.

Sweat is clinging to my back as I make the last turn in the lane leading to the beach club area. I unzip my coat and shake the red *I don't care what Santa thinks, I'd rather be naughty than nice* hoodie from Grandma Dot. A shower of glitter falls from the sweater.

Sticking to the shadows at the side of the road, I slink along. My Charger is parked where I left it. I'd half-expected the tires to have been slashed or some other awful thing to have happened to it, but other than a light dusting of snow, the car is the same as I left it.

The light colored four door I'd seen earlier is parked at the other side of the lot, nearest the beach. I was right, the sticker in the back window is for Barr Harbor Beach Club, the mis-matched rim of the front tire is the same as in my memory. Paula had used her neighbor's car, smart move.

The car is here, but I see no sign of Paula or the kids. An eerie quiet fills the park and beach and marina. The red swing begins moving back and forth, the squeak of the chain unnerving. I turn my back on the odd swing and not knowing what else to do, I go to my car. I lean against the cold metal of the passenger side, putting the Charger between me and the white sedan. I'm not sure what my next move should be.

The cry of a young child tears through the park, carried on the wind from the direction of the marina.

My blood goes cold. The toddler boy. It has to be him.

The kids are here.

With shaking fingers, I pull my phone out of my pocket and text Lucas. I tell him where I'm at, and where the kids are.

He texts directly back telling me they aren't far away, to wait, to not do anything stupid.

The toddler, Ian, wails louder. Cora, the little girl cries out in one sharp exclamation of pain.

I text back, "She's hurting the kids. Not waiting."

A wave of indecision holds my feet to the ground. From the direction of the crying, and the footprints in the snow, I'm sure she's hiding them in the snack shack I noticed earlier. What I don't understand is why she moved the kids. At her house, they were at least under the impression that they were safe and cared for. Now they are scared and crying.

Cora makes another wail, and I can just make out the words. "I want my mom."

The solid sound of a slap against tender skin echoes across the park.

Indecision gone, I open the door of the Charger as quietly as possible. Alexis's gun is still in my glove box. I return the bullets to the gun and double check the safety is on, then slip it into the big front pocket of the Santa hoodie. I pray I won't need it, but a woman who would slap a scared child like that is unstable. It's better if I'm prepared.

I stay close to the lakeshore, hoping to blend in and approach unseen. The very first rays of daybreak touch the clouds with pink. It's Christmas morning and I'm stalking a kidnapper with a gun. Quite a bit different than last Christmas when I woke up with Chester and made him fish shaped pancakes before going to Grandma Dot's.

The snack shack is only a few yards away when the door opens and Paula steps out.

I crouch low near a pier of the marina, hoping against hope, she won't see me.

"If you think I'm dumb enough to not see you, then think again, Gabby."

Her use of my name shakes me. Spotted, I stand tall. "How do you know my name?"

"It took a few minutes after you left for me to put it together. You're that psychic woman who was all over the news about that cult that was selling babies. I remember you."

My "fame" has preceded me.

And has taken away my advantage.

"I know the children are in there. Why?" I ask, actually perplexed.

"The reasons are mine, but let's just say that little tramp was going to keep them from Jared and leave it at that."

"My mom is not a tramp!" The older boy yells from inside the shack. He beats on the door and pulls on the handle, but it's obviously locked.

"You're scaring the kids," I point out. "Why don't you just unlock that door and let them go? I'm sure we can work this all out."

Paula's laugh cracks across the marina and beach. "I already worked it out. In the morning, the kids and I are headed on a long vacation. Later, I'll tell Jared where we are and we can all start over." She inches closer as she speaks.

I don't want to back away, but I find myself stepping onto the pier behind me, the metal planks creaking. "The police are on their way," I tell her. "There isn't going to be a happy vacation or a chance to start over."

Oliver and Cora are now both beating on

217

the door of the snack shack, yelling at their grandma, screaming for help. They are making such a racket, I don't notice the approaching sirens until they are only a few blocks away.

Paula darts her eyes towards the road leading to us, then looks at the shack that is shaking from the children's pounding.

"We want our mom!" The kids shout.

Desperation contorts her face, easily seen in the growing morning sun. She turns her venom on me. "Why did you have to come? The kids were perfectly content until you started beating on my door with that lie about a missing dog."

The wild look in her eyes forces me to take another step back. I slide my hand into the front pocket of my hoodie, wrap my fingers around the gun. I don't want to use it, but the weight of it in my palm is comforting.

"You turned them against you when you forced the car off the road killing Lauren and Eric."

Her face clears into an eerie calm. A ray of sunshine breaks through the clouds and lights up her face with diffuse orange color. She strides confidently towards me, and I back down the pier, knowing full well the metal planks will soon end and I'll have nowhere to go.

From the corner of my eye, I see a River Bend cruiser pull into the parking lot. The siren is off, but the light bar throws blue and red lights all over the expanse of flat snow, marred only by the children's and Paula's footprints.

Paula looks at the car, at the shack full of screaming children, then at me.

I don't like the look on her face, and I turn off the safety on the gun hidden in my hoodie pocket.

After a split second of indecision, she rushes towards me.

I don't want to shoot, but I don't want her to reach me either.

Not knowing what else to do, I pull the trigger.

Chapter 15

GABBY

"Crap on a cracker, that gun is loud," is the thought I have in the split second I have between Paula pushing me off the pier and me crashing through the ice.

My only thoughts after that are for air.

The icy water constricts my chest and cramps every muscle in my body. I'm a good swimmer and kick for the surface. I hit my head on the hard ice, the air I desperately need a scant inch or two away, but unavailable.

I open my eyes underwater, hoping to find the hole I fell through, hoping to find any way to reach the surface that is so close. The water is dark, the early rays of morning sun doing nothing to help me.

I push my hands against the bottom of the ice, pound on it, needing it to crack.

My lungs scream and my mouth desperately wants to open.

I bite my lips closed.

I can not open them, can not open them.

My head swims with lack of oxygen, adrenaline and shock from the cold. I kick and pound and search for the hole.

I listen for direction from my tattoo, but my mind is a jumble.

Under the ice, far in the deep, I see shimmering lights. Globes of glimmer that call to me.

Join us, save us, find us.

The pull towards the lights is strong.

The arm wrapped around my waist is stronger.

It drags me to the surface and my face reaches air.

The glimmering globes are gone, replaced by Dustin's terrified commands.

"Breathe, damn it!"

Chapter 16

DUSTIN

As we race north to Vinton and the Barr Harbor Beach Club, my head feels fuzzy from the pill I just swallowed and the exhaustion dragging at me.

My main concern is for Gabby. Well, not so much *concern* for Gabby. To tell the truth, I'm a bit irritated that again she's gone off on her own and put herself in harm's way, but that's still concern I suppose.

When she finally texts back to us and lets us know where she is and that she's found the kids, concern turns to relief, until the "not waiting" text.

I slam my good hand on the dashboard. "That girl is a menace," I shout. "Good Lord, we're only a few minutes away."

Lucas wisely says nothing, but I can tell he

agrees. He jams the gas pedal harder and the cruiser shoots faster, through the lovely town square of Vinton, IN.

Once we reach the beach and marina area where Gabby said she was, it only takes a moment to realize she's gotten herself backed into a dangerous situation. Paula wears the body language of a woman with nothing left to lose. Gabby is being forced down the pier with nowhere to go.

Lucas and I run towards the women, shouting, "Stop, police."

Lucas draws his gun. Since I only have one arm, I don't draw mine.

Paula advances on Gabby, and a shot echoes across the beach.

I can tell by the sound, that it's not from Lucas's gun.

Gabby falls off the end of the pier and breaks through the ice. For a horrendous moment, I think Paula has shot her.

But Paula is the one bleeding. She holds her upper arm, blood seeping through her fingers.

"The little wench shot me," she says as she runs away across the beach.

Screaming children beat on the shack near the pier.

In the chaos, I shout orders, "Get her, I've got Gabby."

With two good arms, running after and subduing the woman is better left to Lucas. Lucas seems torn, but follows my orders and goes after Paula.

I slam down the pier to the hole where my sister went under, fully expecting her to be there looking up at me.

The hole is empty.

Panicked and terrified, I jump onto the ice, breaking through, smashing the hole to make it larger. My chest hurts from the cold, but I suck down a huge breath of air and go under. With my eyes open, I look for my sister.

I see glowing globes of light that make no sense. Amidst the globes, a dark form that can only be Gabby floats motionless.

I wrap my good arm around her waist and pull her to the surface.

"Breathe, damn it!" I shout. She moans a little. A flood of relief warms my frozen body. I look towards the beach and see Lucas has Paula cuffed and is leading her back to us as quickly as he can. He pushes her down on the ground near the shack.

"Kids, sit tight. You're safe. Just give us a minute to get you out," he says over his shoulder as he hurries down the pier to help me with Gabby. "Is she alright?"

"She's breathing." I'm struggling to keep afloat with soaked clothes and my one good arm wrapped around my sister. Noticing my distress, she grasps a pole of the pier, allowing me to let her go and hold onto the pier myself.

"Hey, Love," Gabby mutters, looking up at Lucas. "Wanna join us for a swim?"

"I'd say she's fine," I say. "Can you get us out of here? It's freezing."

Vinton is not in our jurisdiction, so a local deputy, Cassie Cartwright and her partner Parker Cho soon arrive to take over the scene. Once the children were released from the shack then checked out by the EMTs, we were assured they were at least physically okay. We all breathed a sigh of relief.

Gabby was checked out and also released. Besides freezing our butts off, we were both okay.

By the time the scene was turned over to the capable hands of Cartwright and Cho, I was in desperate need of another pill, a bed and some time with Alexis and Walker.

Social services came for the kids. Lucas and I pushed for them to be returned to their Grandma Teresa, and we were assured they probably would be later today, but for now there were procedures to follow.

Once Jared Whitlow's involvement was confirmed or ruled out, the custody of his children would be determined.

As for Lucas and I, all we wanted was time with our own children.

"Merry Christmas, Detectives," Deputy Cartwright says as we climb into our cruiser. She and Cho wave us good-bye, then approach Gabby at the door of her Charger. They'd already grilled her on her involvement and she'd answered as best she could without giving too much away about how she works. Judging by the pinched look on her face now, they are asking her again.

I actually feel sorry for her. I ask Lucas to stop the car and then roll my window down.

"Gabby, you coming? We can follow each other back to River Bend."

Cartwright and Cho step away and Gabby is soon following us back home.

Chapter 17

GABBY

Staying up all night, nearly drowning and the shock from Dustin saving me has really rattled my nerves. Several minutes wrapped in Lucas's arms settled me down some, but I'm still shaking on the drive home. The heater is running at full blast, but I pulled over and stripped off my wet clothes after we left the Barr Harbor Beach Club. Sitting in my panties and bra on the cold leather seats is a bit chilly.

I'd called Lucas when I pulled over and told him what I was doing. I could tell by his tone that he'd rather be driving with me half naked than with Dustin, but even I could tell Dustin was in no shape to drive right now.

The sun is fully up and it's officially

Christmas morning. I'd called Grandma Dot and Mom to assure them we were all okay and would be at Dustin's soon. They agreed to meet us there.

Olivia and Walker are either already up or soon would be. They would be clamoring to open presents. After everything I went through to get Olivia's presents under Dustin's tree, I want to be there to watch her open them.

Plus, I need to check on Alexis. She was a mess last night and I'm hoping she's better today. I also need to explain to her how I lost her gun at the bottom of Harper Lake. Dustin had asked about the gun, but I lied and said it was the one I took from Grandma Dot a while back. The gun and how I came to have it is Alexis's story, she can tell it when she's ready.

All traces of last night's storm are gone from the sky this morning. The bright blue seems improbable after the snow and ice of a few hours ago. The sun shines warm through the back patio door, bathing Dustin's living room in light. The massive L-shaped couch is full of family, me snuggled up against Lucas's shoulder, wearing some dry pajamas Grandma Dot thoughtfully brought me. Dustin and Alexis are similarly snuggled together on the other end of the couch. Mom sits between us, glowing with happiness.

Grandma Dot, in her usual involved way, is on the floor with Olivia and Walker handing out presents.

Exhaustion pulls at me and I lean heavily against Lucas.

Grandma Dot's excited voice shakes me alert. "Here's one for Gabby, from Lucas."

The small box scares me. Rings come in small boxes.

I love this man, but I'm not ready for a ring yet.

I look at him as I take the box from Grandma's hand. He isn't moving from my side, not heading to the floor to drop to one knee.

I shake the box and hear the unmistakable sound of a chain inside. I give him a huge smile that I hope conveys happiness, not relief.

"Don't look so terrified," he teases. "Just open it."

Ripping off the lovely, carefully taped paper, I open the gift. I lift the lid of the box and inside is a necklace. The dainty silver chain has two stylized hearts linked together. It's romantic, but not cheesy.

"It's perfect," I breathe. "Just perfect."

Lucas helps me put the necklace on and it nestles against my collarbone. I finger the metal, beaming with excitement.

He leans near my ear and whispers so only I can hear, "Not a ring, but maybe next year."

I wrap my arms around him and kiss his stubbly cheek. "As long as I have you, I don't need a ring."

Grandma Dot clears her throat, tactfully reminding me that Olivia is watching.

I remove my arms from him and snuggle against his shoulder again. I take off my gloves and touch the linked heart charm with my bare fingers. A shiver of excitement fills me, caused by love, not my powers.

More gifts are opened and more happiness

fills the room. I drift in and out of sleep. Behind me, on the table near the hall, the elf climbs the ladder, slides down, and then climbs again. The rhythmic sound of the elf combined with the even breathing of a dozing Lucas finally does me in and I fall asleep surrounded by those I love.

The End

Want more exciting books by Dawn Merriman, check out all her books on Amazon.

The other books in this series, in case you missed them, are:
- Book 1, "Message in the Bones"
- Book 2, "Message in the Fire"
- Book 3, "Message in the Grave"

Join Dawn Merriman's fans, on her Official Fan Club on Facebook. Posts from Dawn, discussions about her books, contests, prizes and other fun stuff.

See all Dawn Merriman's novels at Dawn Merriman on Amazon.

Join Dawn Merriman's Newsletter and get a FREE short story at DawnMerriman.com

www.DawnMerriman.com

Other books you will love:

Marked by Darkness.
An intense psychological thriller.

Consumed with grief from losing her husband and children, Maribeth lives alone in a cabin in the woods. Haunted by her dead family and the choices that destroyed them, she just wants to heal. When a woman is murdered and left in her woods, Maribeth can no longer hide. The serial killer who destroyed her life has a copy cat determined to finish her off. Book #1 of the Maddison, IN Supernatural Thriller series.

Field of Flies

A Gripping Psychological Mystery Thriller

Two people want Zoey, dead. One is in her own mind. A quiet, emotionally distressed, pig farmer is sucked into a murder investigation. But closing in on a killer is dangerous. Which is worse - a killer desperate to keep her from finding the truth - or the killer in her mind. Maybe she can stop them both….

A note from Dawn Merriman:

I hope you enjoyed this bonus book about Gabby and the gang. It was a fun book to write. Trying to mix a mystery in with Christmas was a light hearted challenge. Maybe there will be more Gabby books in the future, but I'm making no promises. I have other characters I want to introduce you to that I think you will love just as much.

If you are enjoying my books and would like to stay in touch, I am active on Facebook on an almost daily basis. I post excerpts from my books, funny crime or reading memes and other things related to my author career. Join my Official Fan Club on Facebook. Tell your friends, too. We have a lot of fun on the page. You can also sign up for my email newsletter at DawnMerriman.com and instantly get a Free short story.

If you have enjoyed this book or any of my other books, please take a moment to leave an honest review. Reviews really help.

Thanks for being such a good fan and reading my books.

God Bless,

Dawn Merriman

Here is the first chapter of "Marked by Darkness" Book #1 in the new Maddison, IN Supernatural Thriller series for your enjoyment.

Chapter 1

Maribeth

Living can be worse than death. Death requires no struggle. Death only requires giving in.

Life requires battle, a never-ending succession of skirmishes. Each day an agony of combat, each step a hard-won victory.

Today, my steps of victory crunch through melting snow and piles of fallen leaves. My legs burn, regardless of the cold. This daily run grounds me. I've kept the habit from before the police academy, through my detective career, and now here, one of the few things I kept from my previous life.

I push on through my woods. Trees slide past in a blur. My lungs settle into my pace, my chest rising and falling in customary rhythm. Puffs of steam escape my lips into the frigid air. My feet land on the familiar trail, my legs stretching over downed branches without thought. My body has run this path so many times it no longer needs my conscious thoughts to guide it. My mind is free to roam into the darkness. I struggle to keep my thoughts on the path, to skirt the empty abyss that beckons.

My property consists of three-hundred acres of heavily forested woodlands. When I first came here, the woods seemed to stretch forever, an expansive embrace of trees and wildlife. Now I quickly reach my property line and make the turn back towards the cabin, following the remnants of snowy footprints from my last run.

My only companion, my gray and white husky, Indy, knows the path well, too. As we make the turn towards home, he bounds ahead excitedly, kicking up snow and leaves with his fast feet. Indy stops suddenly, several paces ahead on the trail. He raises his nose to the air and catches a scent. The rabbit flashes across the path and Indy gives chase.

He shoots into the brush, his gray fur flashing against the white of the snow. I watch him go, wondering if I should follow, but I run on. Indy can take care of himself in the woods better than I can. He'll come home when he's had his fill of fun.

The music in my earbuds blasts the last of my dark thoughts about death and life away. I match my feet to the beat and plunge forward one step at a time, eager to get home before darkness falls.

A sharp bark intrudes over the music. I slow my pace, turn the volume down, and Indy barks again.

I pull an earbud out. "Indy?" I call into the trees. A whine and a yelp echo in the stillness.

Panic spurs my feet, and I crush into the brush. One earbud hangs from its wire, bouncing against my chest in a staccato of fear. My breath claws at my chest, hidden branches cling to my feet.

Indy's paw prints lead to a frozen pond and continue onto the thin sheet of snow blowing across the ice. Several yards away, Indy scrapes the edge of an icy hole, desperate to draw himself out of the frigid water.

He yelps in fear, his bright blue eyes pleading for help.

The ice moans beneath my weight as I take cautious steps towards my dog. A crack zigzags in front of me, and the ice gives way. The shallow water bites up to my knees.

Gasping against the icy pain, I push on, breaking the ice with clenched fists. The water crawls up to my thighs. Drowned branches and debris pull at my numbing feet.

Indy watches my slow progress with helpless eyes. The water climbs to my crotch, knocking the air from my lungs as it reaches the sensitive skin.

A few feet away from him, I stretch my arms across the ice, strain to reach the thick fur of his neck. It fills my gloved hand, and I pull. Indy yelps and claws at the ice. One paw catches hold, and combined with my pulling, he slides out of the water.

He crouches on the ice, instinctively spreading his weight on his four paws. He scrambles to the bank and shakes off most of the water. Now that he's safe, he paces the bank of the pond, barks anxiously, spurring me on.

Numbness settles into my bones, making my return to the bank heavy and slow. A submerged branch catches my running boot, tripping me. Icy water clenches around my belly, but I catch myself on the edge of the ice before sinking lower.

Freeing my boot from the branch, I lunge for the bank, pushing hard with my other leg. A hidden scrap of metal slices my foot, the sudden warmth of blood burning against the cold water. Ignoring the pain, I push again for the bank.

I land face down in the dirt and snow, then belly-crawl out of the water. Indy pushes his nose against my face, urging me on with his warm breath. My vision fuzzes, and I shiver in the wind. Using my unhurt foot, I try to stand. My numb leg wobbles, crumples, and I land with a humph. The cold seeps from my soaked legs up to my chest. It slithers under my coat and wraps icy fingers around my lungs.

I will my legs to move, too cold to obey, my muscles only twitch. With my gloved hands, I pull myself through the dirt like an animal. Fallen branches reach out from the snow to scratch my face.

Indy whines and shoves me with his nose, urging. Shadows dance around his broad face, as the sun sinks low in the sky behind him. I manage to drag myself a little farther, then lie panting against the dirt. The cold seeps from my chest into my shoulders.

Indy whines against my cheek. I can barely see his blue eyes in the falling darkness. Behind him, three familiar balls of light appear, and I turn away from their approach.

"I just need to rest," I tell my dog. "Give me a minute."

Music sings softly from my earbuds dragging along beside me. "Dust in the Wind" carries along with the snow on the breeze.

As I have every day for two years, I fight the battle to survive. I don't give in. I don't give up. The cold strikes back, a valiant competitor.

"Maribeth, you have to move," Bryson's voice blocks out the music.

"I can't," I explain to my husband. "Too cold."

"Get up!" he commands. I open my eyes and meet his face.

"You need a haircut," I tell him nonsensically. "You should have gotten one before."

"You say that every time," his warm smile makes a heat flutter in my frozen chest.

"Mom, it's dark," my son, Benny, says from somewhere nearby. "I don't want to be here in the dark."

"I know, baby. Sorry. I stayed out longer than I intended."

"Mom, get up!" My teenage daughter, Lilly, demands. Always headstrong and to the point, she doesn't give in now.

I manage to roll onto my back, and the three of them shimmer above me. The empty branches dance behind them, through them.

"Indy's cold," Bryson says. "You have to get him inside the cabin."

My dog shivers next to me, a crinkling sheet of ice frozen over his thick fur.

"I can't," I whine to my family. "I'm too tired."

"That's the hypothermia talking. Damn it, Maribeth, move!" In our 17 years of marriage or the last two years, I've never heard Bryson cuss at me. "Get your ass in gear and get up!"

I don't like his tone and anger surges through me. When I try to move my leg, it obeys. "That's it, Mom. Screw this shit and move!" Lilly chimes in.

"Watch your mouth, young lady," I snap automatically. Adrenaline pumps against the cold, and I force myself to my hands and knees.

"It's getting darker," Benny fusses, consumed by his fear. "Get us inside."

Even Indy gangs up on me, pushing against my rear. I pant on my hands and knees, crawl a few steps towards the trail. "Why won't you just leave me alone so I can join you?" I plead. "If you had stayed away, I could be with you now." Tears of frustration burn my frozen cheeks.

"You have things to do yet, Maribeth. Now get going." Bryson urges. "Don't let the kids see you like this."

That works more than the harsh words. I crawl a few more feet, then pull myself up on a tree. My cut foot stings as I step down gingerly. "Pain is good," Lilly says. "Do that again."

As blood pumps through my frozen extremities, the skin tingles and burns. "The sooner you get to the cabin, the sooner the burning will stop," Bryson urges.

I pull myself straight and step away from the support of the tree. My cut boot flaps in the snow, but I keep moving, each step agony.

"Good girl, keep moving," Bryson says.

Panting and exhausted, I stop to catch my breath once I'm back on the path to the cabin. I want to sink to it, want to curl up and sleep.

Bryson senses my hesitation and tries another tactic. "Chica and Rizo need their dinners."

"My pigs can eat the grass," I point out.

"It's winter, there's no grass left. They need you."

I look up the dark path where the pigs and chickens wait for my return.

"Just give me a minute," I tell my family and lean against a tree. I dig my pack of smokes from the inside pocket of my coat, and fish out a cigarette. It's squished, but miraculously dry. I fumble with the lighter through my gloves until a tiny flame finally appears. The hot smoke warms my tired lungs.

I take a few drags, summon the last of my energy, and march on.

My family follows, cheering me, pissing me off, whatever they can do to keep me going.

The solar light on my porch finally winks through the trees.

Benny runs ahead, "Come on, Mom, we're almost there."

My pace quickens once the cabin comes into view. In my haste, I trip over a fallen log. Bryson moves to catch me as I fall, but I tumble through his outstretched arms.

After all, he's not really here.

Find out what happens next, get "Marked by Darkness" today.

Printed in Great Britain
by Amazon